Would he reject her?

Kat's heart galloped like a wild horse inside her chest as she held her breath, desperately hoping he wouldn't scoff at her attempt at seduction, though she had to admit, it was a little on the pathetic side. When the heavy silence dragged on, Kat started talking as if her life depended on it.

"I know how this looks," she began hurriedly. "I'm throwing myself at you in some lame attempt at seduction and I wish I could deny it but it's true. I don't know the first thing about being sexy or coy, or how to get a guy to look at me in a romantic way, but the truth of the matter is, there's a good chance I might die soon, and I refuse to die without knowing what it's like to be held and kissed by a man like you."

D1173330

Dear Reader,

If I don't feel a connection to a character, the words simply won't flow. This wasn't a problem for *Moving Target.* Kat jumped out at me from the minute I started writing this story. Her voice and quirky personality drove the story, more so than Jake did, which was a surprise. I guess that's one of the best parts about being a storyteller—you never know how your characters are going to take control. Kat and Jake are an unlikely duo, which is what makes them perfect for one another. I love when characters challenge the other to learn and grow, because it turns out to be one heck of a journey for the reader!

I hope you enjoy *Moving Target.* If you're just coming to this story, you might want to check out *The Sniper,* which is Nathan's story and a great complement to Jake and Kat's story.

Hearing from readers is a special joy. Please feel free to drop me a line via email through my website, at www.kimberlyvanmeter.com, or through snail mail, at Kimberly Van Meter, P.O. Box 2210, Oakdale, CA 95361.

Kimberly

MOVING TARGET

—

Kimberly Van Meter

HARLEQUIN® ROMANTIC SUSPENSE

If you purchased this book without a cover you should be aware that this book is stolen property. It was reported as "unsold and destroyed" to the publisher, and neither the author nor the publisher has received any payment for this "stripped book."

Recycling programs
for this product may
not exist in your area.

ISBN-13: 978-0-373-27860-2

MOVING TARGET

Copyright © 2014 by Kimberly Sheetz

All rights reserved. Except for use in any review, the reproduction or utilization of this work in whole or in part in any form by any electronic, mechanical or other means, now known or hereafter invented, including xerography, photocopying and recording, or in any information storage or retrieval system, is forbidden without the written permission of the publisher, Harlequin Enterprises Limited, 225 Duncan Mill Road, Don Mills, Ontario, Canada M3B 3K9.

This is a work of fiction. Names, characters, places and incidents are either the product of the author's imagination or are used fictitiously, and any resemblance to actual persons, living or dead, business establishments, events or locales is entirely coincidental.

This edition published by arrangement with Harlequin Books S.A.

For questions and comments about the quality of this book, please contact us at CustomerService@Harlequin.com.

® and TM are trademarks of Harlequin Enterprises Limited or its corporate affiliates. Trademarks indicated with ® are registered in the United States Patent and Trademark Office, the Canadian Trade Marks Office and in other countries.

Printed in U.S.A.

KIMBERLY VAN METER

wrote her first book at sixteen and finally achieved publication in December 2006. She writes for the Harlequin Superromance and Harlequin Romantic Suspense lines. She and her husband of seventeen years have three children, three cats and always a houseful of friends, family and fun.

To the real scientists and homeopathic practitioners out there working tirelessly in their lab or garden to find a cure for the dreaded disease of Alzheimer's—your work is important. No one should be made to suffer the indignities of a broken mind. Real heroes don't always carry guns but they always try to save lives. Bless you!

Chapter 1

Katherine "Kat" Odgers fought the urge to cry.

"No," she breathed, staring at her research and back again at the rhesus monkey she'd secretly named Auguste after the first clinically diagnosed Alzheimer patient who lived in the late 1800s. The monkey didn't seem to know what to do with the banana she'd tried to give him. Worse was the fact that he seemed to have lost the ability to do anything a monkey would normally do.

"C'mon, Auguste, don't do this to me," she said, reaching into the cage against protocol. The monkey, frightened, climbed into her arms like a baby and clung to her as if she were its mama. "Oh no, oh no, oh no." She gently administered a sedative and carried the monkey over to a machine geared toward mapping his mental acuity. As she waited anxiously for the machine to do its work, she bit at her fingernails, nibbling at the near-nonexistent sliver of nail, worried and scared—not only for Auguste but for her research.

Had something gone wrong? Had she missed something?

Three years' worth of careful, painstaking research, animal trials that showed brilliant, exciting promise in the area of Alzheimer's research, all hinged on the results of that scan.

The machine finished and after returning Auguste to his cage, she stared at the monitor, reading the results with a sinking heart and a nauseous stomach.

Her drug, MCX-209, was supposed to repair the brain but instead…it had destroyed it.

Somehow she'd missed something crucial, because according to Auguste's scan, the area that stored memory was less wrinkled and nearly smooth in places. His memories had just disappeared courtesy of MCX-209. "I failed," she murmured, tears springing to her eyes as her stare returned to the unconscious Auguste. "And I've ruined poor Auguste."

Bad. Bad. Bad.

She wiped at her running nose and searched for a tissue. She'd been so close. So close to victory over this insidious disease, but now all was lost. Her boss would likely can her for failing so miserably. So much for being a so-called genius. She was so smart she'd found a way to destroy brains without leaving a mark. Brilliant! Yes, she could just imagine the scientific journals already, lauding her for her failure to help a single person suffering from Alzheimer's. Better polish up that résumé, she thought miserably as she collected herself, shuffling to the tiny mirror over the sink.

Her hair hung in its usual disarray, refusing to stay put no matter how many pins she used to try to hold it together. She pushed a strand behind her ear and adjusted her glasses with a disheartened frown as the same face she'd been born with stared back. Not exactly a heart-stopper. As far as career choices go, stripping was not going to be a viable plan B. She had no breasts and she was horribly clumsy, she reminded herself. One attempt at gyrating on a pole would end with someone getting a stiletto in the eye as she careened from the stage, arms and legs akimbo.

Science had been her only gift. And now? Clearly not.

And poor Auguste. He'd been the cutest of the monkeys. Now he was a drooling mess.

She didn't even know if the results were permanent or temporary. Kat blew an irritating strand of hair from her eye. Time to pay the piper. She had to write up her findings and let her boss know that MCX-209 was a total, abject failure.

Jake Isaacs stood respectfully as his superior Miles Jogan walked into Jake's office, his expression stern. "Take a seat," he advised Jake as he dropped a file on

Jake's desk. "I have a job for you—one I would only trust to you even though you're no longer working the field." Jake took the folder and opened it, his interest piqued. "What you're about to read could change the world."

Jake scanned the file, a subtle widening of his eyes the only indication that the information had troubled him. "Who is she?" he asked, regarding the file photo of his subject. At only five feet four inches and one hundred and fifteen pounds—petite—with long wavy light brown hair and very thick black glasses that hid half her face, Katherine Odgers wasn't portrayed in a flattering light. "And why does she matter to the Defense Intelligence Department?" he asked, closing the file.

"Dr. Odgers is the hottest ticket in town," Miles answered, causing Jake to frown. "That woman has just changed the world we live in by creating one of the most dangerous drugs known to man."

"What does it do?"

"The drug, MCX-209, erases memory—permanently. Yet, it leaves other brain functions intact." Miles watched Jake's reaction. As the implications tore like a forest fire through Jake's mind, Miles nodded. "This is why it's imperative that you collect Dr. Odgers and bring her to Washington for her own safety. All other attempts to persuade her have been unsuccessful."

"And what attempts were those?" he asked, taking a second look at the woman in question.

"Naturally, a woman of her caliber would be an asset

to the DID," Miles said. "We made quiet inquiries as to her interest in moving from the private sector to government work but all inquiries were rebuffed."

Jake shrugged. "Government work isn't for everyone."

"It certainly didn't seem to appeal to Dr. Odgers that's for sure. The fact of the matter is, we've run out of time for civil negotiations. We need to secure Dr. Odgers before her work falls into the wrong hands."

"How many people have access to this drug trial?"

"Only her superior, and we've taken care of that weak link." Jake lifted a brow in question and Miles said, "Alive and well but decidedly spotty in recollection of what Dr. Odgers was working on."

"And her research materials?"

"Removed from the laboratory and placed under lock and key. All I need you to do is procure the doctor."

"If she resisted the idea of working for us, what makes you think she's going to want to come with me willingly? Seems a fine line we're walking here."

"Unfortunately, at this point it is necessary to procure Dr. Odgers whether she appreciates the U.S. government's help or not. It's vital that her research doesn't fall into the wrong hands."

Jake knew that sometimes the U.S. government found it necessary to operate under the radar for the good of the people but it always made him feel dodgy when the lines were blurred. And this felt a lot like blurring the lines. "Perhaps she'll change her mind and come willingly after we explain the danger she's in," Jake said.

"We don't have time to hold her hand and hope she makes the right decision. I have it on good authority factions within organized crime and corrupt dictatorships are licking their lips at the prospect of stealing Dr. Odgers's work and using it for their own devices. Our friends in North Korea are quite keen to get their hands on Dr. Odgers, and I can assure you, that will end badly for everyone involved," Miles pointed out with grave certainty. "Including Dr. Odgers."

A drug such as MCX-209 in the wrong hands would certainly upset the balance of power. What if someone drugged the president of the United States with that concoction? Or each member of Congress? A drug like that could ruin the United States of America, reduce it to ash within months as enemies—such as North Korea—jumped at the chance to attack when the country was at its most vulnerable. Jake shuddered at the thought. Even though the mission didn't leave him with a good feeling, he knew the alternative wasn't palatable, either. He nodded to Miles. "I'll leave for San Francisco in the morning," he told him.

Miles offered a tight approving smile. "Bring her straight here. This mission has the highest security clearance. I don't want to run any undue risks."

"Consider it done."

"You're a good man, Isaacs," Miles said. "You do your country proud."

* * *

Kat had just popped a frozen dinner into the microwave when the doorbell rang. Her uncle Chuck would've freaked out if he knew what kind of processed junk she ate these days, she thought idly as she ignored the bell. She'd never quite caught his talent for the culinary arts. Once he was no longer in charge of her meals, her cooking skills had rapidly deteriorated. She liked to justify that she didn't actually have time to spend tinkering in the kitchen but the truth of it was, she just wasn't any good at it. She frowned, glancing at the clock when the doorbell sounded again. Too late for churchgoers on their rounds to convert the masses but not quite late enough for vacuum salesmen trying to wheedle their way into her cramped apartment to wow her with their products' suction power in the hopes of selling one of their exorbitantly priced units. She sighed and wondered if she didn't answer would they go away and bother someone else? They ought to hit up Mrs. Friggen. That old lady would buy anything, and had, judging by the number of times UPS delivered to her door. It was a wonder Mrs. Friggen had any social security left to spend. Kat had a feeling the older woman kept QVC rolling in dough.

Giving up the doorbell, whoever was at the door resorted to knocking forcefully. *Hmm...persistent bugger.* The microwave dinged and she carefully removed the steaming offering of processed cheese and spiraled noodles, her stomach already growling in ready anticipation. As a scientist she knew there was absolutely no nutritional value to what she was about to consume but her taste buds didn't care. She was only two generations removed from Southern white trash, according to the genealogy trace she'd done for fun two years ago, and she loved herself some old-fashioned carb-loading—much to her uncle's chagrin.

She grabbed a root beer to wash her meal down and prepared to hunker in front of the TV and catch up on her favorite DVRed shows—*Renaissance Revelry* was her favorite! But just as her behind hit the recliner, the knock sounded again, only this time, there was a stern voice attached to the incessant pounding. "Dr. Katherine Odgers, open the door or I'll be forced to open it for you."

What? If that was a vacuum salesman, they'd really become more aggressive than she remembered, but the warning tingle in her stomach told her that whoever was on the other side of the door wasn't trying to sell her anything and she wasn't so stupid that she'd comply with their demand to be raped or murdered.

"Go away," she squeaked, trying for bravery. "I have the cops on speed dial. They're coming right now. Run before they catch you. Don't say I didn't warn you. Police brutality is at its all-time high from what I've read in the papers. You better run if you don't want a face full of pepper spray or, worse, a zap from a Taser." She held her breath, biting her lip. Did it work? Where was her cell phone? Drat it. This was her karmic punishment for being so focused on her project that she never remembered where she put a darned thing the minute it left her fingertips. "I swear, they're on their way!" she bluffed, hoping they didn't hear the pathetic tremble in her voice. She shoveled a bite of macaroni in her mouth, burning her tongue in the process but she didn't care. If she was going to die, she wasn't going to go without one last pleasure!

There was a rustle on the other side of the door and she heard the distinct sound of a key slipping into a lock and suddenly she was staring at the super, Henry Willits, as he opened her door for a suit-wearing stranger.

"Henry! What are you doing?" she asked in a strangled voice, unable to believe sweet Henry had just let a possible murderer into her apartment, simple as you please. "What's going on?"

"I'm sorry, Kat, but he's got official business with you that I don't want to get in the middle of," Henry said, ducking his gaze in apology before casting a quick, wary look at the austere stranger. "He says he's from the government."

Kat sat up straighter. "The government?" Her gaze flew to the man who was striding toward her with clear purpose, staring at him with wide eyes. "What are you doing?" she gasped when he stood before her, assessing her boldly and causing her cheeks to flush.

"Your super was kind enough to let me in. Come with me, Dr. Odgers. My name is Jake Isaacs with the Defense Intelligence Department—"

"What's that? I've never heard of such a thing," she interrupted as she stared at him with a mixture of awe and terror. "How do I know you're not making this up?"

Jake pulled his identification and showed it to her. "You haven't heard of us because we operate under the radar. The general public has no reason to know about us."

She found the wherewithal to frown. "That doesn't sound right. Government is supposed to operate with transparency. Are you sure what you're doing is legal?"

He exhaled as if irritated. "I've been tasked to bring you to Washington for your own protection, not embark on a debate as to the ethics of my employer. Your safety depends upon your cooperation, so I suggest you stop arguing and start moving."

"My s-safety?"

"Girl, you'd better listen," Henry advised, looking all of his sixty-eight years, his weathered hands twisting the ring of master keys in agitation. "You in some serious trouble or something."

"She's not in trouble," the man corrected Henry sharply. "But she *is* in danger. Come, I will explain in the car to the airport."

Fly? Oh, no… "I don't fly," she said in a small voice. "I have a ph-phobia."

"That is unfortunate. Nevertheless, you are coming with me."

"I have rights," she said, absurdly lamenting the fact that her macaroni was cooling into rubbery goo. The trick to eating those microwaved meals was to eat them while they were piping hot or else they returned to their previously unpalatable state. "I want to make a phone call," she said, her lip trembling. Wasn't that standard protocol when one was taken into custody?

"Negative," he said, hauling her to her feet as she gasped in surprise. He had a firm grip on her arm as he dragged her to the door while she clutched her macaroni meal and managed to snag her purse only because it was within reaching distance of the front door. She looked to Henry, beseeching his help but old Henry could do nothing, and she had no choice but to stumble after the mean man until he stuffed her into an awaiting black town car with no offer to allow her to pack or grab a toothbrush.

"Is this some kind of joke or prank?" she asked, shrinking against the leather upholstery of the sleek vehicle as they navigated the dark San Francisco streets like a predator in the night. "Someone put you up to this, right?"

He spared her a short glance, his angular jawline illuminated in the moonlight slanting in from the window. "I assure you, this is no joke. There's a price on your head for creating the world's most dangerous weapon in recent history. You are being taken into custody for your own protection until such time as the government can decide how best to proceed."

"There has to be some mistake," Kat protested in shock. "I don't make *weapons,* I swear to you. I'm knee-deep in research for the cure for Alzheimer's. I promise nothing I've done is to hurt anyone."

"Are you not Dr. Katherine Olivia Odgers, social security number 321-65-3498, employee of Tessara Pharmaceuticals, badge identification K-O-O-1183, birth date—"

"Yes," she cut in, openly horrified that a total stranger had access to her most sensitive data. "But I didn't create a weapon! My most recent experiment ended in failure. Surely, you have the wrong person."

"Did you create drug MCX-209?"

Kat drew back, blinking. "Yes."

"Then you're the right woman. Your drug—whether you deem it a failure or not—is now considered a drug more dangerous than every bioweapon out there."

"That's impossible," Kat whispered, shaking her head. "MCX-209 was never created for any purpose aside from healing the brain. Everything was going really well until Auguste forgot how to be a monkey."

"Be that as it may, the potential ramifications of such a drug in the wrong hands are too catastrophic to leave unchecked."

Good gravy. This was how people got brutally murdered in the movies. They took long rides in black cars and their loved ones never saw them again. She glanced down in despair at her shabby sweatpants and ratty UCSF sweatshirt and lost whatever shred of composure she had left as pure terror took over her mind. "Are you going to kill me?" she cried, her nerveless fingers dropping the cold meal onto the floor. She sucked in a breath as macaroni bounced off her toes and landed on the vehicle carpeting. "Oh! Gross," she whimpered before burying her face in her hands to sob. "I'm going to die with processed cheese on my feet! This is so not fair!"

"Stop crying," he instructed her, curling his lip at her rising hysterics; but she didn't care.

"All I ever wanted was to help people, to help my uncle fight that insidious disease and now I'm going to die because I inadvertently created a weapon of mass destruction!" she wailed, staring morosely at the mess at her feet as she hiccupped. "And I didn't even get to eat my macaroni!"

Of all the ways she thought she might go out…this wasn't even in her top five.

Chapter 2

Jake wanted to clap his hands over his ears at the woman's incessant wailing but he fought hard to remain composed, gentling his voice as he attempted to calm her. "No one is going to kill you. You watch too many movies if you think we're driving to your doom. The whole point of taking you into custody is to protect you from people who might not feel the same as the United States government." He was pleased to see his words had penetrated her wailing for she slowly calmed down and peered at him through wet lashes. "I promise you, you are safe," he assured her.

"Are you positive?" she asked, her voice nasally and small. "You're not just saying that to get me to be quiet? So that I'll go docilely to my own demise?"

"Well, there is that—the *quiet* part," he muttered,

then added hastily when her eyes widened again, "Of course not. That's not how my branch of the government works. We're going to board a private plane to Washington, D.C., where you will be properly protected while we sort this situation out."

"Oh." Her mouth made a small o but just when he thought he'd calmed her sufficiently, he realized her teeth were chattering. At his perplexed expression, she reminded him plaintively, "I'm terrified of flying. I mean, *massively* phobic. I might even pee my pants if you try to put me on a plane."

He released an irritated sigh. "Then I'll give you a light sedative. You will go to sleep and wake up magically in Washington."

"Yeah, that seems logical but I'm allergic to most sedatives. I found out the hard way about that. Makes getting my dental work done a challenge."

Was she kidding? He narrowed his stare. "This is no joke. I don't have time for games."

"Why would I lie about an allergy?" she asked, frowning.

"To get out of flying."

"I'm really not lying…about flying." She broke out into a tiny smile at her inadvertent rhyme, then apologized when she realized he did not find the humor. "How far is it to drive to Washington?"

He glowered. "Too long. At least two days of hard driving with minimal stops."

"I've always wanted to go on a road trip," she admitted with a shy smile and he had to stop himself from growling. She shrugged at his expression. "I'm just saying, a drive could be nice."

Nice? Driving cross-country with a jittery scientist did not sound nice at all. But what choice did he have? He was tasked to bring her to safety and that's what he would do. He didn't care if he had to charter a bus to do it.

"Driving it is, then," he agreed, but then added, "This is no pleasure cruise. We are not sightseeing or stopping for tourist attractions. It's going to be a blur of truck stop diners, convenience store bathrooms and endless driving until we reach our destination."

"You should work for Travelocity," she grumbled, but nodded. "Okay."

Jake realized in his haste to procure her, he hadn't actually allowed her to pack any clothes. He groaned, knowing what her next request would be so he said gruffly, "We'll stop at a Target before we hit the road so you can pick up some provisions."

"Oh, good!" She looked plainly relieved and he felt like an idiot for not allowing her to prepare properly. However, in his defense, he'd thought they were going to fly and they would've been in Washington within six hours. After he'd delivered her to his superior, the department would've seen to her needs. Now? It was his job. He shuddered as an odd sensation twanged his insides.

"Is this your first government kidnapping?" she ventured, and he bristled.

"No, and you were not kidnapped."

"I've never been kidnapped before but I imagine being forced from your home without a choice in the matter is a lot like being kidnapped," she reasoned, adding almost cheerfully, "but what do I know? I spend eighty percent of my time enclosed in a lab with rhesus monkeys for company. I might actually enjoy the human interaction."

"Perhaps you could find a book to read while you're in Target," he suggested, not liking the idea of fielding questions from this oddball chatterbox.

"Oh," she said, taking the hint. For some reason, he felt like a cad for shutting her down but he stiffened against the feeling. He wasn't her tour guide or her bosom buddy. He was a government employee, fulfilling his duty. End of story. Feelings of any sort did not play in the mix. And yet, his mouth fought to utter some sort of apology. However, she saved him from stumbling through an embarrassing attempt when she recovered quickly to quip, "Well, as cute as monkeys are they don't actually talk back so I'm accustomed to having full conversations with a relatively silent partner. No book required."

Oh, Lord…this was going to be the longest ride of his life.

Kat tried not to squirm, feeling the silence in the car like a suffocating blanket tossed on her head. She risked a glance at the man who'd plucked her from her apartment without so much as a polite conversation to buffer the abrupt change in her circumstances and wondered if she were suffering from Stockholm syndrome because to her eyes, he was quite handsome. His dark hair was cut with precision, without a single hair out of place, which, of course, made her intensely aware of her general state of dishevelment, and his clothes were crisp and foreboding, as if he was dressed by the costume director of *Men in Black*. She plucked at the dingy sweats she always slipped into once she was safely behind her own walls and dropped all pretense of trying to fit in. Why couldn't she have at least worn something a little less unflattering?

"I can practically hear you thinking," he said, sighing. "You don't have to worry. No one is going to get to you now that you're in custody. Rest assured, the U.S. government has your best interests at heart."

She started, realizing he'd misinterpreted her consternation but she had to laugh at his last comment, saying, "Even I know that the U.S. government doesn't do anything that doesn't benefit the government in some way. But that's not what I'm thinking about."

"Oh. Why were you frowning?" he asked.

"Because I look like a house frau." *And you're so damn handsome that you're making me feel like a drab, little mouse.* She shrugged, rubbing at a dark stain on her sweats. "And I wished I'd been wearing something a little less…frumpy."

"Comfortable clothes are best for traveling," he said

sternly. "No sense in getting prettied up just to sit in a car for hours on end, right?"

She smiled, warming to the fact that he'd attempted to put her at ease, which she sensed was not in his nature. "True," she agreed, and returned her gaze to the dark landscape as it zoomed by. "So, how long have you been married?"

Jake shot her a quick look, alarmed. "Excuse me? I'm not married. What gave you the impression I was?"

"Because you're so handsome," she answered simply. "You know, I've worked with a few government employees before when Tessara landed some contracts with the U.S. government but none looked like you and I think I created a stereotype in my head that they all looked like pudgy, balding salesmen in cheap suits."

"Even the women?" he quipped dryly, and she laughed.

The corners of his lips played with a smile, which only made him sexier, and she realized that she was inappropriately attracted to this austere man.

Definitely Stockholm syndrome.

"You didn't answer the question. Why did you think I was married?"

"Oh, because someone as good-looking as you doesn't stay single for long. Even if you were gay, some smart gay guy would snatch you up pretty quick I'm fairly certain. You're not gay, though, are you?" He shot her a dark look and she took that to mean he preferred women, not that she had a chance with someone like him. He was the quarterback and she wasn't even the bookish nerd in the library. She was that really strange girl who liked to chew on her hair and formulate algorithms for fun. "Sorry for the personal questions. When I'm nervous, I tend to ramble and I have difficulty determining social boundaries. I was tested for Asperger's but the results were inconclusive. Either I have it and I'm really good at fooling the test, or I don't have it and I'm just weird."

"You don't seem that weird to me," he offered.

"That's because I'm holding in most of my weirdness. If I were to let it out…you'd probably drop me off at the first bus station. Once, a blind date excused himself to the restroom and never came back. To be fair, I knew from the start we weren't compatible but he'd been so cute that I'd overridden my initial reservations to at least get through dinner but it hadn't mattered, he'd left me at the restaurant. In my experience, monkeys have better social skills than people because at least they don't lie."

"Not everyone lies."

"All humans do," she disagreed easily, but she didn't blame him for his opinion. She wasn't passing judgment, just offering a statement of fact backed up by historical evidence. "It's an evolutionary protection for the species."

"How so?"

"Well, lying was the first built-in protection measure. To deflect consequence, which oftentimes was death. Noblewomen lied all the time to keep their heads on their shoulders. If a woman gave birth to a female rather than a male heir—somehow it was her fault even though men determine the sex of the fetus. And if a male was sterile, it had to be the woman's fault so she got herself knocked up by the stable boy and passed it off as her husband's child. You'd be shocked at how many royal babies were actually born on the wrong side of the blanket—" She stopped short when she realized Jake had checked his rearview mirror three times during her explanation. "Is something wrong?" she asked, turning around but he stopped her with a curt instruction.

"Keep talking, and don't look back. Someone has been following us since we left your apartment. Act natural."

"Act natural? What does that even mean? You just told me that I was safe and now you're telling me that someone is tailing us? Wouldn't that, by its very nature, preclude the concept of safety?"

"You are safe. They are behind us, not in the backseat."

"They who?" Her neck ached from remaining unnaturally stiff. "Who is following us?"

"I don't know but I can't imagine they have your best interests at heart. Remain calm while I reason this out."

"I think I'm going to tinkle," she moaned, admitting, "I have a nervous bladder, too."

"Well, whatever you do...don't tinkle. This car is a rental."

Jake pressed his foot on the accelerator and Kat's fingernails dug into the armrest as she squeezed her eyes shut. "I used to dream of something exciting happening to me but I take it back. I don't want excitement. I want my boring, uneventful life back." She lurched forward as tires squealed and Jake whipped into some pretty amazing defensive driving skills. In spite of being told not to, she jerked around to peer out the back window and got blinded by headlamps that seemed pushed up their tailpipe. "Did they hit us?" she asked in a horrified screech as the realization that they were in real-life bumper cars nearly caused her to lose her bladder control right then and there. She clamped her thighs together and prayed, and while she was at it, she took back every fevered whisper she'd ever uttered in the misguided hope of becoming something more than a nerdy scientist girl who still hadn't lost her virginity!

Chapter 3

Jake had no idea who had hooked in behind them but he'd noticed the vehicle tailing him about a block after leaving Katherine's house and he knew they were in trouble. He gritted his teeth and wrenched the wheel to whip down a side street, then took another sharp turn down a street in a zigzag manner in the hopes of losing the tail.

"I don't want to die like this!" Katherine wailed, her fingers clutching the "oh, shit" handle for dear life. "Dying in a heap of twisted, burning metal was not how I thought it would all end!"

"No one is dying today," he bit out, pushing the town car to go faster. "But whoever is behind us is pretty damn good behind the wheel. I can't seem to shake him!"

"You said you'd keep me safe. I don't feel safe! I don't feel safe!" Katherine cried, screaming when he skidded around another corner, narrowly missing creaming a fire hydrant. "Just let me off at the corner and you can continue your car chase without me. I'm done with all this government stuff. This is what I get for letting a pretty face override my good sense. I knew I shouldn't have left with you."

"Katherine! Shut up," he demanded, wishing he had a sock to stuff in her mouth. "I can't concentrate when you're screaming like a banshee."

She buttoned her lip but her eyes were wide as saucers behind those ridiculously ugly glasses and he felt a pang of remorse for snapping at her but he didn't have time for much else if he wanted to get them out of this jam alive. He didn't know San Francisco well enough to navigate with the speed he needed. He flipped the navigation system on and barked at Katherine. "Can you read a map?"

That seemed to jerk her out of her funk and she scowled as if he'd just asked if she could operate a toaster. "Of course I can read a map," she answered with a glare. "I'm not stupid."

"Then *navigate*. I don't know this city well enough to know where the dead ends are. We need to lose this tail or we're going to run into some serious problems."

"Fine! But stop snapping at me and stop calling me Katherine. I prefer Kat, if you don't mind."

"Fine! *Kat.* Get on it!"

"Take a right down Landers," she shouted seconds before he passed the street. He jerked the wheel and they skidded down the narrow street, clipping a parked car and smashing a taillight. "And then hook onto Fourteenth. If we can lose him long enough, we can catch the 101 from there."

"Sounds like a plan to me." He drove dangerously fast down the residential street and prayed they didn't hit a pedestrian or attract the attention of a beat cop. The last thing he needed was to involve local authority. Fate smiled on them and their tail didn't catch their last-minute switch down Landers. Jake booked it to Fourteenth and within minutes, the freeway entrance loomed. The town car's springs groaned as they jounced along the uneven pavement of the centuries-old city and they took the freeway access like a bullet exiting the chamber. The town car hurtled down the freeway and melted into the night.

Kat couldn't breathe. She'd always been a weak, spindly thing as a kid and as if that hadn't been bad enough, she'd been afflicted with asthma, too. She'd mostly outgrown it but there were times when she had flare-ups, usually when she was under extreme stress or after cardio activity. Since she still hadn't grown much stronger since high school, she didn't see the point of going to the gym and since being in her lab was soothing, she didn't have all that much stress. But one wild car chase was enough to awaken her sleeping breathing disorder and now it seemed her body wanted to take a nostalgic walk down I Can't Breathe Lane. Her chest fought to draw air into her aggrieved lungs but they were being stubbornly uncooperative. "J-Jake," she managed to gasp, her vision dotting. "I—I c-can't b-breathe…"

"What?" Jake shot a questioning look at her and immediately took the off-ramp. "Do you have asthma?" he asked. At her jerked nod, he swore under his breath. "Concentrate on remaining calm. You need to focus on drawing breath into your lungs. I'm guessing you left your inhaler at your place," he asked rhetorically, chagrined. "Okay, hold on. Caffeine will work in a pinch."

He screeched to a stop at a convenience store and dashed inside. He returned with an espresso in a can and helped her drink. "The caffeine will dilate your lungs enough to calm down," he explained as she struggled to quell the panic. Her fingers shook as she gripped the can with his help. Bit by bit, the caffeine started to loosen her lungs and she took slow, measured breaths with relief. He removed her glasses carefully and wiped away the tears that had trickled down her cheeks.

"Feeling better?" he asked, his gaze searching hers. She nodded, her heart rate finally slowing to a normal speed. She struggled to sit up, but he wasn't about to let her move too quickly. "It's okay. We can take a minute. We lost the tail miles ago. Why didn't you tell me you needed your inhaler?" he asked.

"I forgot. It's not every day that I get kidnapped for my own good. I forgot my toothbrush, too."

"You haven't been kidnapped," he corrected her with a subtle frown.

"If I haven't been kidnapped, am I free to go home?"

"You know it's not safe there," he answered, his frown deepening. "This incident just proves my point. Whoever was tailing us had been minutes from your apartment. Something tells me they weren't coming over for tea."

Kat worried her bottom lip. It was difficult to refute plain logic. "So now what?" she asked.

"First, we need to ditch this car. They'll be looking for a rented town car."

"Especially one with a smashed-out taillight."

"Yeah, that's true, too."

"So…that returns us to my original question. What are we going to do now? If I had a car, I'd offer to drive but it's too darn expensive to park in the city. I take the BART or the Muni to get around."

"We couldn't take your car, anyway. Chances are whoever was tailing us would've already received intel on your vehicle and would've been looking for it. We'll rent a car."

She peered at him, enjoying the faint tingle at the pit of her stomach as she perused his handsome face. Up close, she could smell his cologne and the warm scent of his skin. So masculine, she noted almost clinically. From an evolutionary standpoint, he'd make lovely babies. "You really owe it to the human race to pass on your genes," she mused. She clapped a hand over her mouth at his look of astonishment, then realized she had no choice but to own it. "You have to know you're very handsome. I'm just saying that the world loves a pretty face. You won the genetic lottery. Do you have a brother?"

He scowled. "Yes, but he's taken," he answered, misinterpreting her reason for asking.

"Not for me, you goose. Just wondering if your parents spread their beautiful DNA among a sibling group. For the good of ensuring pretty people inherit the earth, of course," she tried joking but he didn't laugh.

At the mention of his parents, his expression became shuttered and all semblance of tenderness or concern fled from his eyes as he pulled away. "Are you feeling better?" he asked.

Sharing time was over, apparently. "Yes. Thank you. I never knew that trick with caffeine," she murmured, sharply disappointed in the change.

He nodded and pulled away from the parking lot to ease back into the flow of traffic. "I need to make some calls. We'll hole up in a hotel for the night and then start fresh in the morning."

"Okay," she said, risking another look at Jake. Her assessment still stood. Her kidnapper was one beautiful—and judging by the way he freaked out when she mentioned his parents—emotionally screwed-up individual. Her good sense said to steer clear but his messed-up psyche called out to hers and she was help-less to resist it. She'd always been a sucker for the bad boy with the broken heart, even if the bad boys in her past had never even looked twice her way. In her imagi-nation, she'd nursed plenty back to emotional stability wherein they became productive, emotionally selfless individuals capable of mature love and admiration. Did she mention she was alone with her thoughts a lot in her youth? *Aaaaand, this is why I'm still a virgin,* she thought dryly.

"For the record, men aren't pretty," he stated, his eyes never leaving the road. "Only women and little girls can be called pretty."

"Really? I never realized there was a rule in effect." She paused then said, "Babies are pretty."

"No. Babies are, at best, cute. But most look like doughy old men until their hair grows long enough to discern gender. Women are pretty. Men are handsome," he explained gruffly. "How would you feel if someone called you handsome?"

She smiled wistfully. "I don't think I'd mind much. Anything aside from 'four-eyed weirdo' would be a pleasant change. Unlike you, as you can see, I didn't exactly win the genetic lottery." She tried for light-hearted self-deprecation but it still stung to know that she was no swan and deep down there still remained the seventeen-year-old girl who wanted the cutest guy in school to notice she was more than someone to copy chem notes from.

"You're not ugly and anyone who would say so is plainly blind," Jake said, shocking her. He shook his head as if befuddled they were even having such a conversation, and gestured to the navigation. "Find us a cheap hotel off the main streets—something old and less likely to be filled with tourists. We need to be as low profile as possible."

Kat swallowed the questions that had bubbled to the surface at his shocking statement and nodded, her mind chattering. Did he, in a roundabout way, just call her pretty?

A slow grin lifted her lips as delight tickled her insides.

Sounded like it to her.

Jake, her government protector/kidnapper, thought she was pretty!

She'd take it.

Chapter 4

They'd been driving for hours. Or maybe it just felt that way because her stomach had been grumbling for the past hundred miles and she was ready to start chewing on the upholstery if she didn't get some food pronto. "I'm new to this kidnapping thing but is food on the agenda? I have a very high metabolism and I have a tendency to burn through calories at an alarming rate. If you recall, I was in the midst of my dinner when you kidnapped me for my own good."

"Will you stop saying that? I did not kidnap you. Government officials do not kidnap people."

She shrugged. "I'm not going to argue semantics with you when I'm too hungry to temper my words."

"Why do you think you have to temper your words?"

"Well, you carry a gun, you're kind of surly, and I'm not sure you like me, so under the circumstances, I would say it's probably wise to temper my words. But I'm starving and you're starting to look as good as a ham on rye so it's very possible my judgment isn't the best right now, which means I may well say something I probably shouldn't."

"I get the picture. You're hungry," he said dryly. "Do you have any dietary restrictions I should know about?"

"I don't care for sweet potatoes," she answered, thinking. "And I'm not wild about cucumbers. It's not that I don't like the taste—they're okay—but I'm a little uncomfortable with phallic-shaped vegetables." Was that a snort? She cast him a sidewise glance but found him watching the road, stoic as ever. Perhaps she'd imagined it. "And I guess the same goes for bananas but I do eat them because they're good power foods."

"Power foods."

"Yeah, you know, foods that digest slowly for the maximum fuel benefit for your body. I'm surprised you don't know about that considering how fit you are."

Was that a tiny smile playing at the corners of his mouth? Oh, it was, which told her he'd been playing her. "You know all about power foods. You're probably the kind of person who only eats raw, organic and brings their own utensils to a restaurant."

"Hardly. Just because I believe in eating clean doesn't mean I'm OCD. But yes, I already knew about power foods. I was just surprised you know about them."

She frowned. "And why is that?"

"Because when I picked you up you were about to eat a bunch of processed goo masquerading as macaroni and cheese."

Kat sniffed. So judgmental. "I happen to like that processed goo. I'm a scientist and adhere to the better-living-through-chemistry creed. And unless you grow everything you eat, you can't afford to be so *judgy*. There are chemicals everywhere." She risked a short glance his way. "Do you grow a garden?"

"A small one," he admitted reluctantly. "Tomatoes, bell peppers and cucumbers mostly—the nonphallic kind. And when I asked about your dietary needs, I meant, are you allergic to anything?"

"No." Of course he was. And she'd started talking about her weird little food quirks. He must think she was a nut-ball. Heat burned her cheeks but she lifted her chin and tried to return the conversation to something somewhat normal. "Well, good for you. I have a black thumb. I have a tendency to kill anything green. Back to the original topic, can we please, for the love of all that's holy, get some food before I pass out?"

He had MREs but in the interest of time, perhaps a drive-through would be best, he realized.

"In-N-Out work for you?" he asked with a sigh and she nodded gratefully. Jake maneuvered the car across the lanes and took the first exit with the huge In-N-Out sign sticking out over the freeway. "Good. We're using the drive-through."

"Actually, a potty break would be great." At his dark scowl, she shrugged. "I can't help the way the human body was created. Gotta eat and drink, gotta go number 1 and number 2. Simple biology. Don't like it, take it up with evolution. Or God. Whichever way your philosophies swing, it doesn't matter to me."

"Fine." He exhaled and pulled into a parking spot. "But we're not dallying. You relieve yourself while I order the food. What do you want?"

Relieve herself? He sounded so formal. But she supposed that was efficient. "Cheeseburger, animal-style."

"Animal-style?"

She smiled. "They'll know. Secret menu."

"Right," he said, looking at her as if she'd dropped a screw. "Animal-style it is. Anything else?"

"Medium—no—make that large soda and fries. I'm starving."

He gave her a look that said he didn't know where she would put all that food. It was a look she recognized because people often gave her that look. She could put away an entire large pizza on her own within an hour or two. When she returned from the restroom she found Jake sitting by the window, watching the parking lot warily. From this vantage point, he had a clear visual of the car. "Do you think they're still after us? And who exactly are they? Russians? Are we still in conflict with the KGB? Or maybe the Libyans?"

"You don't get out much do you?"

"No. Not really." She spent most of her time in the

lab or in her apartment without much deviation, except on occasion she ventured out in costume for cosplay conventions. Should she mention that? He probably didn't even know what that was. Some people thought cosplay was weird. She didn't want to run the risk of coming off as totally strange, so she added instead, "Sometimes I attend renaissance festivals."

"Is that where they dress up and pretend to be from the Middle Ages?" he asked, and she nodded, even though he'd gotten the time period wrong. He followed with a short grunt. "Why?"

"I like the costumes and the history." Plus, just like cosplay, it was fun to pretend to be someone else for a day.

"And who do you dress up as? Queen Victoria?"

She scowled. "I see history was not your favorite subject in school. Queen Elizabeth I was a Renaissance queen, not Queen Victoria. And no, I don't dress up as the queen. I'm a…fairy princess."

"Fairy princess?" He nearly choked on his burger. He wiped his mouth when he could breathe. "I don't recall fairies being somewhere in history."

"Not all participants follow the actual history. It's just fun to dress up," she retorted, her cheeks heating. Now she definitely wasn't going to tell him that she also enjoyed dressing as Catwoman at cosplay conventions. She liked the feel of the latex and it made her feel bad-ass when she'd never actually been badass in her life.

And it was sexy…another thing she'd never considered herself on a normal day.

She stuffed down the urge to reveal such a personal thing about herself and instead, changed the subject. "So…who are the superpowers these days?" Jake refrained from immediately answering and dug into his burger instead. She took that as a cue to continue talking but awkward silences were…well, *awkward*. "It's a bit weird to wrap my head around what is happening," she said, munching her fries. "I mean, the most excitement I've had in a long time is when my apartment super installed the new dishwasher. I really hate hand washing. It's not the actual washing of the dishes that bothers me, it's the way my hands feel after they've been stuck in water for so long that the skin prunes up. Ugh. I hate that feeling. It always feels like I'm rubbing together two pieces of wet parchment paper."

"Wet parchment paper would rip," he said between bites and checking his watch.

"Okay, maybe not parchment paper but something other than human skin and that creeps me out." She took a big bite and Jake's eyes widened imperceptibly but she was used to it. She had a big mouth and she could cram a lot of food into it. "So where you from?"

"You should concentrate on swallowing your mouthful. You might choke."

"Sorry," she said, realizing she needed to brush up on her manners. Spending time with monkeys wasn't all that good for social interaction with humans. "Forgot." She swallowed her mondo bite but couldn't stop talking. "My uncle raised me when my parents died and he didn't have a single clue about raising a little girl but he tried real hard. So I'll try not to do anything terribly, inadvertently offensive in the future." There was a minute roll of his eyeballs and she pursed her lips. "You could use a brushup on your social skills, too, you know. If we're going to be traveling together, we should at least pretend to get along, right?"

"Why?"

His blunt response took her aback. "What do you mean, why? Because that's what nice people do. They pretend to get along until such time that they can talk about each other behind their backs later. It's called civilized society."

"I thought you said you don't get out much? How would you know what civilized society does or doesn't do?" He didn't wait for an answer and shoved another fry in his mouth, saying, "We're not friends and we're not bound to be friends anytime soon. You represent a mission and I will see to it that you are safely delivered as per my directive. Understand?" At her dejected nod, he seemed satisfied and continued eating. "We leave in five minutes. I don't feel comfortable being out in the open like this."

Well, poop. So much for making the best of things and looking forward to an impromptu road trip. Tears stung her eyes and she had to look away before she embarrassed herself. Too late. Jake had noticed and he probably noticed what an ugly crier she was, too.

"Are you crying?" he asked.

"No." A tear slipped down her cheek and she wiped it away. "And what difference does it make to you if I'm crying or not? I'm just a *mission,* right?"

"Oh, criminy," he muttered, his dark brows pulling into a frown. "Look, I didn't mean to hurt your feelings. I just don't want to give you the wrong idea or anything."

"Like what? I know I'm not the kind of woman a man like you is going to notice. All I was hoping for was a little conversation. For the past three years my life has been consumed with the clinical trials of MCX-209 and the most scintillating conversation I've had has been a one-sided debate with a rhesus monkey." She hadn't meant to reveal so much about her lonely life but the information had pretty much spilled from her lips like a tipped-over beaker, leaking all over the place. She scrunched her trash and grabbed what was left of her burger, needing to get out of there. "Let's go. We can eat on the way. No sense in dragging out this mission any longer than we have to."

And before Jake could really see her cry, she bolted for the car, leaving him to stare after her.

Jake wasn't sure what had just happened or how but one thing kept snagging his brain. He'd completely crushed her feelings somehow and it bothered him. Her feelings mattered to him, although they shouldn't. How many missions had he accomplished without a second thought as to how the target felt? Too many to count. And Kat certainly wasn't his first female target, either, so what was the problem? He crunched his trash and tossed it, sighing as he followed in the direction Kat had gone. He'd assumed she'd gone to the car but when he found the car empty, alarm spiked his blood. Damn it. He scanned the parking lot and saw a Target adjacent to the fast-food restaurant. Double damn. They didn't have time for Kat to go shopping but he supposed if it stemmed the tears, he'd let it slide. Besides, as she'd said, she needed a toothbrush. He wasn't a complete jerk. Maybe this would prove it to her.

Who cares? It was better if she believed him a jerk. He didn't need a target trying to get chummy with him. Entanglements clouded judgment.

But as the minutes ticked by, he knew he couldn't wait any longer and trotted toward the store to collect his wayward charge. He found her easily enough by narrowing down the various locations he could expect her to be in. As luck would have it, he found her in the undergarment section. Jake controlled his gaze and said, "Next time you take off, let me know where you're going. On second thought, no more taking off on your own. We have no secure locations at this point until we get to Washington. Got that?"

She nodded and stuffed what appeared to be a pink thong and panty set into her basket under the small pile of toiletries. But he could still see the pink frill peeping out from beneath the shampoo and conditioner and his imagination inexplicably began processing what Kat would look like clad in nothing but that piece of frilly nothing. "Do you have what you need?" he asked more forcefully than he intended but she didn't seem to notice. In fact, she seemed to be on a mission of her own and pulled that lingerie out to dangle in front of him. "What are you doing?" he asked, a tad alarmed.

"I don't know," she admitted, but her eyes were wide as she added, "But I want your opinion on which is better." Then she grabbed the black bra and panty set still on the rack and held them up to compare the two.

He averted his eyes as if scalded by the sight, which was plainly ridiculous. This was not the first bra and panty set he'd seen. Hell, he'd removed quite a few with his teeth and nothing more. But somehow having Kat ask that question threw him for a loop. "This is highly inappropriate. I must ask you to refrain from asking such personal questions that do not adhere to a certain level of propriety." Before she launched a protest, he strode forward and pulled the ugliest, most utilitarian granny panties from the rack and thrust them at her saying, "These are more appropriate for our trip. They are functional and they won't ride up your backside at inopportune moments."

Kat bit her lip and accepted the ugly white drawers, then broke out into an unexpected smile. "Good thinking. I think I'll get both. The pink and the white.

A girl should have variety. Thanks, Jake." And then she stuffed the undergarments into her basket and began walking to the checkout lane as if they were a normal couple out for a quick shopping trip and not a government official protecting a woman in jeopardy.

Once they were back in the car, Kat turned to him and said, "I'm sorry for that freak-out back there. When I'm under a lot of stress I tend to act out inappropriately. It's one of my quirks, I guess. Once before midterms in college I was so stressed I started singing songs from *My Fair Lady* in the middle of the cafeteria. I'd read once that singing could reduce stress levels and what started out as a tune hummed under my breath suddenly became much more than that."

"You must've been under a lot of stress," he murmured as he maneuvered back onto the highway, but his mind was stubbornly stuck on those damn panties. Was he losing his touch? He lived his life under a certain code and that code included honor and integrity. Allowing an attraction of any kind to a target compromised the mission and he'd never allowed it to happen. Not once. Not even with a Russian model! Olga had been all legs and hips and cunning womanly wiles but he hadn't even blinked an eye at her charms. But Kat? Awkward, gangly, too thin, nearly blind if her thick glasses were any indication of her visual acuity, *she* was doing strange things to his resolve? He rubbed at his eyes. "We need to find a hotel for the night," he said. Maybe sleep would straighten him out. If not, he had bigger problems.

Chapter 5

It was nearing midnight and the only motel available with any vacancies was a small, ugly and dubiously habitable place in the middle of nowhere. Whereas Kat's impression wasn't favorable, Jake found it perfect.

"They probably have bedbugs and all manner of vermin," she said fearfully. "Or those pincher bugs, you know those ones with the things on their heads and they look like they could chop your finger off with one little click…please tell me we're not staying here."

"Sorry. But this fits our needs. We need something that would likely be overlooked by whomever is chasing us. No one in their right mind would stay here."

"Exactly. And I'm one of them. I'm not saying I'm high maintenance or anything but typically I like my beds to be free from creepy crawlies."

Jake cracked a short smile. "One night will not kill you." At her horrified expression, he added, "Don't worry, I will check to make sure your bed is free of creepy crawlies."

They entered the '70s-era lobby that smelled of old carpet, cigarette smoke and bad choices, and he couldn't help but notice Kat sidling closer to him as if she were afraid something nasty or contagious was going to latch on to her leg. He tried to ignore the urge to pull her closer if only to reassure her that it was going to be all right. Piped in elevator music—the kind that made you want to plug your ears and grit your teeth—played in the distance, probably from another room and after two sharp raps on the ringer, a fossil of a man teetered out of the back room. The man's balding pate revealed brown age spots and broken blood vessels here and there and Jake wondered if the man was senile. "Two rooms, please." By the expression on Kat's face she didn't want to spend a night alone and as luck would have it, she got her wish.

"Only one room available. But it's got the fancy tub that the ladies seem to like." The old man winked at Kat and she blushed a telltale shade of red at the insinuation. "Unless you only want to rent the room for the hour. We can do that, too."

At that Kat sputtered, "By the hour? We're not those kind of people, you old horny goat."

"Oh, honey, in my day I christened every single bed in this joint but that was a long time ago," he said with a regret-laden sigh. "My rutting days are all but over at this point."

"And to think I was worried about bugs, not geriatric DNA," Kat muttered, and looked away with obvious distaste. For a split second Jake considered looking for something less disgusting but it was late and he was tired, but he did make a last-ditch effort to procure two rooms. "Are you telling me that this place is so full you only have one room available?" he asked, incredulous. "I find that hard to believe."

"I didn't say we were full. I said we didn't have but one room. Does this look like the Taj Mahal to you? The rest of the rooms were shut down by the health department. So alls we got is the one room. Got it?"

"Let's just keep looking for someplace else," Kat urged, tugging at Jake's shirtsleeve as she cast a fearful glance around the dismal surroundings. "This place is disgusting and it gives me the creeps."

Jake agreed with her and it wouldn't have been his first choice if he were on a normal mission but there was someone on their tail and until he found out who, he would take no chances. He hesitated before sliding his credit card across the counter as it would be the easiest way to track them but he took a calculated risk in that whoever was on their tail didn't know who he was yet to track his personal cards. Besides, he didn't have much choice. He didn't have enough cash on him to pay for the room. "We'll take it," he said firmly. Kat made a sound behind him like a groan and he smothered a grimace. The old man swiped his card and handed over a key.

"If the crapper gets plugged up there's a plunger in the room. And sometimes the hot water goes out after ten minutes so don't be taking all night in the shower unless you like cold showers." The old man shot a look at Kat as if his warning were meant for her and then shuffled back from whence he came. Jake pocketed the key and directed Kat back outside and down the shotgun alleyway of rooms to the one he'd paid for. Jake turned the key into the lock but the door stuck when he tried to open it. He gave the door a hard push and it came free with a sticky sound. "Don't try to figure out what made the door sticky. It'll just make for an even longer night," he advised Kat as he walked inside. The room was as ugly as the front lobby, not that he expected anything different but from what he could see it seemed relatively clean. However, the one problem that was immediately evident was right smack-dab in the middle of the room.

"There's only one bed," Kat observed with a tremulous tone. "And I'm not sleeping on the floor."

One look at the threadbare carpet and he wasn't, either. He propped his hands on his hips. "Okay, so we sleep together fully clothed. Problem solved."

"I can't sleep with pants on. I get claustrophobic because I can't move freely."

If Kat hadn't looked so miserable in her admission he might've barked at her to stop complaining and just do as she was told but he couldn't. She was a terrible actress and her misery was printed very plainly on her face. He softened for her benefit. "All right, so we share the bed," he said, adding, "I want you to know that you are safe with me. I would never touch you inappropriately. We can successfully sleep in the same bed without anything improper happening."

"I'm not worried about that," she said with a mild frown.

"Then what are you worried about?"

"Do you snore?" she asked.

"Not that I'm aware. How about you?"

"No, but sometimes I talk in my sleep."

That didn't surprise him. The woman couldn't stop talking when she was awake. "I'll find a way to deal with it. Would you like the bathroom first?" he offered solicitously. She nodded and scooped up her bag of Target items and disappeared behind the closed door. Except…the door didn't entirely close. In fact, if he looked at just the right angle he could probably have a narrow view of everything that was going on behind the partially open door. He sighed and closed his eyes deliberately. A tingle of awareness hit him in the groin region and he was disconcerted by his body's reaction. It was baffling. Kat was nothing like the women he was usually attracted to.

Determined to regain focus he pulled up his emailed notes on his phone and then sent a quick email to his superior informing him of their minor run-in with whoever was trying to kidnap Kat. Five seconds later his phone rang and it was Miles. "Do you have the scientist?" he asked brusquely, going straight to the point, but Jake didn't take offense. A mission this important required focus, not idle chitchat.

"Of course. I have secured the target but we've had to deviate from the plan because she's afraid of flying and allergic to anesthesia."

"How allergic?"

"Pretty allergic. And I didn't want to risk it."

"Of course, of course. So you're driving from California to Washington?"

"Affirmative."

"What is your location now?"

Jake hesitated, something in his intuition told him to withhold sensitive information due to the lack of security in the airwaves. "We're safe for the night. I will contact you tomorrow with an update. Hopefully I'll know more about who's chasing us. In the meantime any intel you could provide me is appreciated."

"I don't like not knowing where you are but I understand. I know you're a good operative and you will maintain your objective against all odds. This is why I put you on the job, Jake. There's too much at stake to let that scientist fall into the wrong hands. Her research would be devastating in the hands of an opposing political power."

"I understand, sir. I will do my best."

"I know you will."

The line went dead and Jake clicked off. Connecting with base reaffirmed his focus. The bigger issue was keeping Kat's research from falling into the wrong hands and he needed to remember that. Kat might not be the most beautiful woman on the planet but the knowledge inside her brain made her the most valuable woman to the United States and he would protect her with his life.

Jake kicked his shoes off and lined them up neatly at the edge of the bed, a habit he retained from his military days and, after double-checking the door was locked, he wedged the single chair in the room up against the door handle. He heard the bathroom door open and the smell of steam, fruity shampoo and clean hair followed. He turned to tell her she could take the right side of the bed but the spit dried in his mouth. Glasses gone, and her hair braided off to the side and draped over her shoulder, Kat stood there in that pink frilly bra and panty set, looking unsure of herself and wholly unaware of how incredibly sexy she was. "What are you doing?" He could barely get the words out.

"I don't have any pajamas," she said. "And I didn't want to put on dirty clothes when I was clean. This was all I had. I was going to buy pajamas at Target but you showed up and we had to leave."

Good God, he could not sleep next to her if she were going to look like that. Already his penis was stirring like an eager teenager on a first date. He turned abruptly and grabbed his bag, pulling out one of his T-shirts and tossing it at her. "This should work. Please put it on."

There was a long silence and he risked a second glance her way. She was looking forlornly at the shirt and he realized he must've hurt her feelings again. But he couldn't risk the mission by doing something stupid and fueled by hormonal urges. He was highly trained and skilled in controlling his body, and one awkward, inexplicably sexy scientist would not derail him. "Is there anything else you require?" he asked.

"I must seem pretty pathetic to you, right?" she asked.

Why would she ask such a question? "Of course not," he answered, taking care to avert his gaze from her delicate body. Everything about her seemed delicate and highly breakable, from her lean body and completely cuppable breasts. "Let's get some sleep," he suggested. "We have a long day ahead of us tomorrow."

Kat disappeared into the bathroom and returned a second later wearing his T-shirt. But it was then he realized he'd made an even bigger mistake. How was it possible that she looked ten times more the seductress in his simple white T-shirt than she had in that pink frilly getup? Sweat beaded his brow but he did his best to remain impassive. He waited for her to climb into the bed and then he followed, ensuring that he kept a cushion of distance between them, and then he turned off the light. He lay there, rigid—in more ways than one—and he was thankful for the darkness. What a fraud he was. If she knew that his entire body was as hard as an oak, particularly the downstairs region…Jake would never live it down. Well, he just had to make sure that it never happened again.

A small voice in the back of his head whispered, *Good luck with that,* and he knew this mission was going to leave a mark.

Chapter 6

Kat turned away from Jake and rested on her side, staring into the darkness, wide-awake. Her insides crawled with mortification at what had just happened. She must've looked like a boy in girl's clothing with how few curves she actually had. What had she been thinking buying that pink getup? It'd been so beyond her comfort zone.

Truth be told, she preferred men's boxers to girly panties, mostly because her uncle, being an older bachelor with absolutely no experience in raising children, much less young girls, had been disconcerted by the idea of such fripperies that he had given her boy's underwear from the start. And frankly, she'd discovered they were far more comfortable than girl's underwear, anyway.

What would Jake think about her wearing boxers? The look on his face was seared on her brain. Had he been disgusted? She was so inept when it came to the social etiquette of attraction and how to act on it. She was a genius in the lab but a total idiot in the real world. What was she thinking? The circumstances were highly irregular but given that there was a tangible sense of danger and there was something about Jake that made her insides light up like a Christmas tree with twelve strands of Christmas bulbs, she hungered for something that was just out of reach. She knew it wasn't right because the situation they were in was bananas but she couldn't help the way she felt. Kat tossed around and punched her pillow, swallowing a groan when her brain wouldn't shut up.

"You need to get some sleep," Jake murmured, adjusting his pillow. "Morning will be here before you know it and we're hitting the road at first light."

"I would love to sleep. I'm jealous of people who can fall into bed and manage REM within seconds. I'm not hardwired that way. Sometimes, *a lot of times,* I suffer from insomnia," she admitted.

"Just do what you do at home to get some shut-eye."

"Not possible. I get up and work mathematical equations until I fall asleep."

He yawned. "Count sheep."

"I've never understood the counting sheep thing. Why sheep? Why not orangutans or giraffes?"

"Because orangutans and giraffes don't jump fences. Now close your eyes and go to sleep."

If only it were that easy. She'd never slept with a man before. It was weird to have someone else in the bed with her. She could feel his every movement, could hear his slow and steady breathing. And if there was anything less relaxing she didn't know. "Tell me something about yourself," she suggested. "Maybe that will help me sleep."

He exhaled as if trying for patience and said, "What would you like to know?"

"Anything. We are strangers sharing a bed—that's not normal in my life. Maybe if I knew a little bit more about you I'd be less nervous."

"Do I make you nervous?"

"All men make me nervous. Well, no, that's not entirely true. Certain men make me nervous."

There was a pause. "And I assume I fall in the category of 'certain men'?" She nodded even though he couldn't see her head bob in the dark. "What kind of men make you nervous?"

"Handsome ones," Kat squeaked out, her cheeks heating. Thank God for the darkness. "Ones that are built like Roman gods."

He barked a short derisive laugh. "Roman god? I can see my choice to limit carbs has paid off."

Kat smiled at his quip, hanging on his every word

uttered in the darkness. Somehow it seemed less threatening to speak her mind when she was sheltered by the dark. She rolled to her back.

"I'm flattered," he continued. "I think. But there's no need to be nervous. I told you I would never take advantage of my position."

She bit her lip, wishing she had the guts to admit that she wished he would. *That would be terrible,* she admonished herself, but the hormonally soaked libido she hadn't even known was there, seemed to be in charge. "I know you wouldn't do anything shady. I already told you that's not what makes me nervous."

She heard the frown in Jake's voice as he asked, "Then what makes you nervous?"

"It's a self-esteem thing that you wouldn't understand."

"Try me."

"Okay, I'm willing to bet you were pretty popular in high school."

"Not particularly," he said, surprising her. "I lived on the fringe of everything."

"No sports? You know, football, baseball, basketball—the trifecta of organized sports in high school?"

"Nope."

For a long moment, she remained in stunned silence. "Oh." She'd just applied a stereotype and found herself corrected. "I'm sorry...I just assumed because you're so confident and fit that you probably ranked pretty high in the social hierarchy of high school. The teenage arena is usually dominated by people like you, or as I should say, the exact opposite of someone like me."

"Which is?"

"Geeky, socially awkward, into math and science… the chess club."

"I like chess."

She smiled again. "Me, too."

"I wasn't popular. Up until my senior year, I was quiet, small and clung to the shadows. I spent most of my high school career trying to disappear."

"Why?"

"Because invisible people don't get hit."

"Were you bullied?"

There was a minute pause before he answered with a short, "Yeah," and Kat sensed a wealth of unspoken pain beneath that single word. Jake inhaled a long breath and turned on his side away from her. "No more story hour. Get some sleep."

Kat listened to Jake's breathing and knew the moment he'd dropped off but it was a long time before she followed him into dreamland.

The following morning Jake rose before Kat and showered, needing the jolt of water against his face to clear his head. Last night had been strange and not because he'd been sleeping beside a relative stranger. He should've been sleeping with one eye open, a catnap of sorts that conserved energy but kept him mentally aware. The exact opposite had occurred—he'd slept like the dead—and if he wasn't careful, he'd end up really dead by making costly mistakes like that.

He scrubbed his body quickly and efficiently but even as his movements were sharp, his brain felt dull and fuzzed. It was Kat. Something about her tilted him upside down. What was with the story-hour sharing episode? He never shared snippets of his childhood with anyone. It's not as if his childhood had been filled with happy warm-and-fuzzy moments worth sharing. He could sum up his childhood in one word: *miserable*.

It'd been the yearning in Kat's voice that had prompted him, something in her voice had pulled the confession right from his mouth like a fish reeled from a line. No more of that, he told himself sternly, tucking the towel around his torso and exiting the bathroom to find Kat awake and waiting. She hopped from the bed and smiled briefly before mumbling something about "needing to tinkle" and maneuvering around him to close the door quickly behind her. He heard an audible sigh of relief as the faint noise of "tinkling" followed and he allowed the tiniest of grins before shaking his head at how bizarre it was that he found her ridiculously...adorable.

In a completely irritating way, of course.

He dressed quickly, saying to the closed door, "Stay put. I'll be right back," and went to the car to get some food. He returned with two MREs. He preferred the military Meal Ready to Eat when on a mission. They were fast, nutritious and immediately ready. He could fuel his body within minutes and continue on his mission without losing valuable time. Kat emerged and her gaze fell on the brown packaging designated for her and she grimaced at her choice. "Meatloaf for breakfast? I've eaten some strange things in the morning but never a military-issue meatloaf package. Is it good?"

He shrugged and ripped his open, wasting little time. He didn't even bother to check the flavor or meal choice. "They're serviceable. I've never had one make me sick. Eat up. We need to hit the road within the next fifteen minutes."

"Can't we just hit a donut shop along the way? I could use a coffee."

"Negative. I warned you this wasn't a road trip. We need to make serious tracks and that means no meandering into donut shops."

"I'm not asking you to meander anywhere. I just don't want to eat that. Most people don't choose to eat an MRE. It's meant to keep you alive and that's it."

"Exactly." He didn't see the problem and spooned a heaping bite of whatever was in front of him. He thought it was meatloaf but upon tasting it, he wasn't sure. Either way, didn't matter—it kept his stomach from yowling. "Come on, let's go. We're on a tight schedule."

Kat opened her MRE with distaste and eyed the contents with suspicion. "My uncle Charlie would die if he saw this," she murmured. "He loved creating culinary masterpieces in the kitchen and I'd been his willing taste tester. Even his disasters had looked better than that meatloaf."

"Be that as it may, it's meant to sustain you, not win blue ribbons for its aesthetics. Try it. You might like it."

"Not likely," she grumbled, but took an exploratory bite. He was about to praise her for giving it a shot when she gagged, wiping her mouth with the back of her hand. "No way. I can't," she declared, shaking her head resolutely. "I will lose whatever is left in my stomach if I try to eat that."

"You can't eat this but you can eat that disgusting macaroni Frankenfood?"

"Yes. My uncle didn't approve but I loved that Frankenfood, thank you very much, and although nutritionally your MRE might be superior, at least the Frankenfood tries to preserve the illusion of being edible by making it taste good."

"You're being ridiculous," he said, scooping up the last of his meal. "But it's your choice to go without. I should warn you, lunch is a long ways from now."

"You are absolutely refusing to stop for anything else?" she asked.

He answered by stuffing his trash in the wastebasket by the door and shouldering his pack. "I'll be back in five minutes. Be ready to leave."

When he left, Kat was eyeing that MRE as if it were the enemy. Hey, at least she wasn't eyeing him the same way, he thought with a smidge of humor. His good humor didn't last long, however, when the unmistakable ping of a bullet burying itself in the wooden post barely missed pegging his head. He ducked and spun away on instinct, taking cover and immediately scanning the direction of the shot. Damn. His calculated risk had backfired. He cursed under his breath. The only person he'd made contact with was at headquarters, which meant whoever was out there had tracked his credit card. Or maybe the rented town car, with its busted headlight, had tipped them off. He knew he should've ditched it right away. He swore under his breath at the costly mistakes he'd made thus far. He pulled his gun from his waistband and waited. When nothing happened, he took a tiny step in the direction of their room and another bullet shot exploded the glass behind him. Jake took a shot in the direction he thought the shooter was hiding and then bolted for the door, slamming it shut behind him.

"What's wrong?" Kat asked, a spoonful of her meatloaf midway to her mouth.

"Guess you lucked out. There's no time for eating. Someone's discovered our location and they are trying to ensure that we don't leave without an escort."

"How'd they find us?" she asked, swinging her legs over the bed to dress quickly. "I mean, do you have some kind of tracking device implanted in your skin or something?"

He cut her a short glance and answered, "No," but he suffered the knowledge that he'd been the reason they'd been found. He had three scenarios, one more likely than the other two. The credit card had been traced, someone on the inside of his department was crooked and had used the department's resources to hunt them down or the car had been spotted, leading them to this roach motel, which, given how remote the place was, seemed unlikely but he couldn't discount the theory altogether. His intuition was screaming something he didn't want to consider. Seemed highly suspect that the minute he made contact with headquarters, a sniper was suddenly aiming for his skullcap. He wasn't so naive that he thought his department was immune to corruption but he hated to jump to that conclusion without solid proof. Besides, it seemed a long shot that someone within his department was crooked but a niggling doubt wouldn't shut up.

"Maybe they're tracking your cell phone?" she suggested, frantically stuffing her belongings into the Target bag. "I mean, all smartphones are equipped with GPS nowadays, right? I don't actually have a cell phone because I don't have a long list of people I would consider calling, unless you consider the pizza delivery man applicable. Come to think of it, I don't have a list of people at all—"

"Kat...be quiet," he ground out, and she sank back on her heels with an embarrassed nod. "Stay away from the window," he told her. "We need to get to the car but they're going to expect that. I saw another car parked in the back that I think belongs to the proprietor. We'll borrow his and leave the town car."

"How are we going to do that?" she asked.

"We're going to climb out the back window of the bathroom. I already checked last night and it's big enough to climb through."

She frowned. "Why would you do that? Were you thinking of escaping in the middle of the night?"

"Always check for two exits when you stay somewhere. Basic survival skill."

She shaped an exaggerated O with her mouth and nodded. "Okay. I'll follow you, then."

He backed away slowly from the window and went to the bathroom, wasting no time in pulling his specialized Swiss Army knife, which contained more than the usual scissors, blade and file. He shattered the glass with the glass punch and the old glass tinkled to the ground.

"That's handy," Kat observed with interest. "Where can I get one of those things?"

"Special issue," he answered, pushing the broken glass clear of the pane with a rolled-up towel, then gestured to her to hurry. "Let's go. With any luck whoever is out there didn't hear the glass break but if they did, they're going to figure out real quick our plan."

Kat approached the window, shaking her hands. "This looks a lot easier in the movies," she admitted, shooting Jake an uncertain look. "What if I get stuck or something?"

"You won't. It's big enough for us both to clear, now get moving. I'll be right behind you."

"I'm starting to wonder if I should've chanced the

anesthesia," she grumbled, and he couldn't have agreed more. Flying would've been a hell of a lot easier.

"Too late now," he said, helping her up to the window. She cleared the pane to jump to the ground a short distance below. Jake landed soundlessly beside her and gripped her hand to run.

The ancient Camaro looked equal parts rust and nostalgia but Jake didn't have time to be picky. He slid into the driver's seat and ripped the wires beneath the column to kick-start the old classic muscle car, and it roared to life with only a mild sputter to clear its throat. "Not bad," Jake said, flashing a grin at Kat. "It's a shame a car like this is owned by a fossil like him. This baby's got some life in her."

"Great! Then burn some rubber already!" Kat suggested. He agreed, flooding the car with gas and spewing rock and dirt as he cranked the wheel and sped out of the parking lot. No shots rang out behind them but Jake knew they were far from in the clear.

Chapter 7

"Do you think they're following us?" Kat asked fearfully, glancing behind them and scanning for a rapidly approaching vehicle trying to climb up their exhaust pipe. Seeing nothing but average everyday traffic, she looked to Jake for answers. "I don't understand. How did they find us?"

"I don't know," he answered curtly, but she sensed he was holding back information. Did he think she couldn't handle it? He continued, watching the road with a critical eye. "You might be right about the cell phone," he said, fishing his cell from his pocket. He handed it to her. "Punch in this code at the opening screen—7863."

She did and watched as the screen started to melt away. "Whoa. What just happened?"

"Internal self-destruct. Now toss it from the window."

"But that's littering," she protested with a frown. "I can't just litter. That goes against my promise to limit my footprint."

"Isn't that a little hypocritical of you?" he asked. "You work for a pharmaceutical company. The chemicals they work with aren't exactly earth-friendly."

"Well, I know. But I try to mitigate what I do personally to bring about the total destruction of the planet. Although I suppose you have a slight point." She exhaled unhappily and tossed the phone, wincing at the faint crash and shatter they left behind. "I'll have you know that one action puts me at square one with my 'days pure.'"

"Do I even want to know what that means?"

"It means I've gone 1,260 days without littering. Not even a wad of gum."

"That's great. I'm sure the earth is grateful."

"Your sarcasm says otherwise." She sniffed. "Someone has to care about the earth. My uncle was really big on the green movement. When he was coherent, that is."

There was the slightest hesitation before Jake said, "Your uncle has Alzheimer's, right?"

"Yes." God, she hated that word. When someone had Alzheimer's, they no longer existed as anything but an old person with a broken brain and that killed Kat. Her uncle was more than a broken brain. He was her only family and the only living person who had ever looked out for her. Her uncle had been her universe. But no one knew that because they didn't think to ask anything beyond that simple word.

"That sucks," Jake said, but he said it in the way that most people did, as if they were simply offering what was expected of them when faced with something tragic. It probably wasn't fair to judge them for their attempt at social etiquette but Kat found herself more and more snarly when offered such stale platitudes. "Must be rough," he added.

At her stiff silence, he said, "For what it's worth, I think it's pretty noble of you to dedicate your life to researching a cure."

"It's not noble at all," she disagreed with a touch of heat to her words. "My reasons for aggressively going after a cure are entirely self-serving."

Jake did a double take. "How do you figure?"

"Because I don't care about anyone but my uncle getting better and I spent three years of my life trying to perfect a drug that was never going to work, anyway. And worse, it's something that can be weaponized. I should've spent the last three years trying to find a cure for cancer."

"Hey, don't beat yourself up for going after something that's near and dear to your heart. That's how people find results—it's the passion to succeed that makes the impossible possible. You have a reason to fight. You have a reason to keep going when all signs point to failure. Don't apologize for what fuels your passion.

You're a freaking genius, girl. I wish I had half your brainpower. You have a gift and a talent that you were meant to use for the greater good."

She stared, unable to believe what Jake had just said. She took back her snippy internal thought about flimsy platitudes and how useless they were. Jake actually cared. Why? She didn't know but the sentiment felt wondrously warm and cuddly up against her heart. "Thank you," she said, not sure what else to say. An awkward silence followed but she didn't feel compelled to fill it as she normally did. No, maybe it wasn't awkward silence at all. Maybe…it was just silence. The car rumbled down the freeway, eating the miles, and Kat settled against the stiff vinyl seat. Her nose tingled at the sharp scent of aging car and cold seats and she let the silence take over as she drifted into a memory.

"How about some warm milk, kiddo?"

Kat had only been seven when her parents died in a freak skydiving accident in Brazil and Kat had been trundled off to her bachelor uncle, Chuck, her mother's distant, older brother. She'd been tired, scared and grief-struck by the time she'd been dumped off with Uncle Chuck and a little punch-drunk. Uncle Chuck, a burly man with a thick, salt-and-pepper beard that hung from his face like a puffy Brillo pad, had taken one look at Kat and as he'd put it, "softened like butter left in the sun."

"I'm lactose intolerant," came her small answer. "It hurts my tummy and gives me the tooties."

Uncle Chuck had thought about her answer and rubbed his expansive belly, saying, "Hell, maybe that's my problem, too. Sometimes I get the tooties, too, when I drink milk." She cracked a tiny smile and held tightly to her teddy bear. "How about some cookies and juice, then?"

She nodded and followed her uncle Chuck to the old faded kitchen and scooted into a wooden chair at the table. Uncle Chuck brought the cookies and they sat that first night, eating cookies and drinking juice, getting to know one another, bonding over a tragedy. To this day, when she needed comfort, Kat turned to cookies and juice.

Kat closed her eyes, wishing she still had that teddy bear to hold on to but, more important, wished her uncle were still available to eat cookies and drink juice with over a hard day. Jake may think her noble for chasing after a cure but right about now, she didn't feel particularly noble—only the fresh stabs of grief for failing her uncle when it mattered most.

Jake knew something was eating at Kat but he thought it best to leave her be until they were safe again. When he pulled off the highway, she perked up to ask, "What are you doing? Bathroom break? I hope so. I'm about to wet myself."

"Not exactly. We're making a pit stop until I can get something figured out," he answered, maneuvering the car onto a side street and then down an isolated dirt road.

"Pit stop? Where?" she asked, watching as the signs of civilization receded. "We're not heading for another dirt motel are we? I'm not sure I can take another of those."

"No, we're going to my brother's place," he answered. "Nathan owns a cabin out here to go target shooting. It's miles of nothing but trees and dirt and there's no one who can sneak up on us without us seeing them first."

"Is your brother nice?"

"Nice? What do you mean? That's an odd question."

"No, it's not," she returned, affronted. "Well, if he's anything like you, then that answers my question."

He did a double take. "Did you just space the fact that I saved your life back there?"

Kat appeared loath to remember that but relented with a short, unhappy sigh. "Sorry," she said. "Being on the run with an emotionally constipated man is murder on the manners." Kat seemed to realize that comment was also mean and tried to make amends, saying, "I'm sorry. I shouldn't have said that. You're right, you did save my life and I appreciate the fact that I'm still breathing, though if you continue to shove MREs in my face, I might consider that a particularly vile form of torture."

"I told you this wasn't a pleasure trip."

"Boy, you weren't exaggerating."

A surprised smile tugged at his lips but he squelched it when he remembered what had started this conversation. "What's with all the questions about my brother?

She shrugged. "Just curious."

"Why?"

"Because I thought if you told me a bit about your brother, I could learn more about you."

He frowned. "I've told you everything you need to know about me."

Kat glared and he got the distinct impression she wanted to bop him over the head with something blunt. "Why do you get so prickly whenever I ask anything remotely personal? Are your past, present and future considered classified information? Are my questions a threat to national security? Geesh, I'm just trying to get to know you. Don't you think it might be easier to handle this little adventure if I felt a little more secure about the man in charge of my safety?"

He hated to admit it but she had a small point, but he didn't know which bits and pieces of himself were safe to share, without revealing too much. Frankly, he didn't trust the feelings that kept bubbling up without notice when it came to Kat and her unorthodox personality. She had a way of getting things out of him that no one else had ever done before. That, in of itself, was frightening to a guy like him. "It's not a good idea to get too chummy," he said and her expression fell into a disappointed frown that did terrible things to his resolve. He exhaled a short breath and against his better judgment, said, "We're not close so I don't know much about him."

"Must be nice to have a brother, though."

How did he respond to that? "I guess."

"You guess? Is he a jerk or something? How do you not know your own brother? Did you grow up apart?"

"No, we grew up together but..." Hell, here's where the words dried up. He couldn't tell her what happened in his childhood, how his brother had left him behind in a war zone where kids were not only collateral damage but the target, as well. He didn't reveal that part of his childhood to anyone. Much less to a virtual stranger who did weird things to his head. "I don't like talking about my past. Okay?" Was that a note of desperation in his voice? She made an exasperated sound as if his answer made no sense. "Then why are we going to his place?"

"Because I know I can trust him."

"You do realize you're talking in circles, right?"

"How so?"

"Because you're not close but you trust him? Don't you have to be close to someone to trust them?

Jake considered that and then shrugged, not willing to dig any deeper into that mucky pool of thought. "Either way, those are the facts."

"Your childhood must've been interesting to say the least."

"*Interesting* isn't the word I would choose."

"What word would you choose?"

"Brutal."

There he went again, blabbering sensitive information. Jake wanted to stuff his own fist in his mouth. "Listen, I can hear the questions forming in that supersmart brain of yours. This is all I'll say about the matter…my childhood was dark, bleak and filled with bouts of pain and misery. My father was a drunken bastard and my older brother split the first chance he could get, leaving me behind to bear the brunt of the old man's fury. Got it? Paint a good enough picture?"

"Yeah," she answered with a solemn nod. "I'm sorry."

"Don't apologize for something you didn't have a hand in." She surprised him with a sudden laugh. He scowled. "What's so funny?"

Kat sobered quickly. "Nothing. It's just that I found it ironic that I was irritated at you for offering a platitude and then here I go doing the same thing to you. I apologized because it felt as if I should because my childhood was different."

He could see her logic…as crazy as it was and grunted his acceptance and moved on. "So, here's the thing, Nathan is a decent guy and we recently helped each other with something he had going on, and I think he has the right connections to help me find out who's trying to cut us down before we get to Washington."

"You think they're trying to kill us?"

"Actually, probably not you because you're valuable. I'm simply in their way and expendable."

She shuddered. "And what exactly would they do with me if they managed to catch me?"

"I doubt they're trying to invite you to tea, if you catch my drift. Torture to achieve their means is not a far-fetched possibility."

She gasped. "Torture? Aren't there rules against that sort of thing?"

"Honey, laws only apply to those who follow them."

"So much for the Geneva convention," she muttered, and he smiled.

"Well, you're not exactly a political prisoner, either, so that wouldn't apply, anyway."

Kat exhaled a long breath. "I'm so not good at this on-the-run thing. I never realized how attached I am to the simple pleasures of sleeping in my own bed and soaking in my own bathtub, not that my bathtub was anything to write home about but at least it was mine."

"I'm sorry," he said, and he meant it. She'd been dragged into a pretty messed-up situation through no fault of her own. "I'll do my best to get you to safety as soon as possible."

"Thank you," she said, breaking into a short-lived smile. "But you and I both know my life isn't ever going to be the same. How am I supposed to go back to life as it was when someone, somewhere will always know about the drug I created? I would imagine someone is always going to want it."

He couldn't lie. "You're right. Likely, you'll get a

new identity and you'll have to start life someplace else, doing something else."

"Like what? I'm a scientist."

"I don't know but I'm sure they'll think of something appropriate."

She sighed and laid her head against the window. "I liked my life just the way it was, which is strange to say now that I realize how much I'm going to miss it. I used to wish I had a different life. Something more exciting or adventurous, even though I can't fly, I have stress-induced asthma and I don't actually know how to interact with people socially…but I guess it's human nature to want what you don't have. Except now I want what I used to have back. Does that make sense?"

"It does," he admitted, surprised that her dizzying logic didn't completely confuse him. "For what it's worth…I'm sorry."

"Yeah, I get it. There's nothing you can do about it. You're just following orders."

Jake shifted against the discomfiting feeling that squeezed his heart at the faint dejection in her tone. He didn't like knowing that it bothered him. He was getting too close to her, that much was apparent. "Glad you understand that," he said, returning his focus on the road and ignoring the sharp stab of something that felt a lot like denial.

Chapter 8

Jake kept his eye on the rearview mirror, watching for anything that looked remotely suspicious but thus far the drive to Nathan's place had been smooth sailing. His brother's cabin was just outside of Reno, up in the mountains. The only reason Jake knew about the place was because a few months back, Nathan and his girl, Jaci, had been caught in a bad spot and if all hell was going to break loose, Nathan had instructed Jake to hide out there. It hadn't come to that—thank God, everything had worked out with minimal scarring—but it'd been a close call.

He'd nearly lost his brother on that mission. He'd been surprised to have conflicting feelings about that, seeing as Nathan had abandoned Jake to enemy territory when Nathan had split to join the marines. Nathan had promised to come back for him. Yeah, well, that didn't happen. No one rode in to save Jake. Not Child Protective Services, not a single neighbor. He'd saved his own hide. Hell, if he'd waited around for someone to rescue him from that hell, he'd have ended up buried in the backyard.

And so, yeah, he had conflicting feelings about Nathan. On one hand, he missed his older brother, but on the other? He wanted to punch him in the mouth.

As if keying in on his turbulent thoughts, Kat asked, "Is your brother going to be there when we get there?"

"No. But I know where he keeps the spare key. I'll call him as soon as we get there."

"I know I made that snippy comment earlier, but I'm really curious…are you and your brother anything alike?"

He scowled. "Why? He has a girlfriend."

Kat laughed. "Calm down, I'm not looking for a date."

"Why do you want to know?"

"Because you fascinate me and I can't seem to help myself from wanting to know more about what makes you tick."

"And my brother plays into that, how?"

She shrugged. "I don't know. I didn't have any siblings and always wished I'd had one. You have to admit, you're an enigmatic sort of guy. A tantalizing mystery always begs a little digging."

"Enigmatic, huh?" Was he losing his mind that he found that flattering? Or was it that *she* thought he was enigmatic that he liked so much? He shifted with discomfort at his own internal dialogue.

"We're nothing alike," he finally answered. That probably wasn't true. Jaci had said they were exactly alike but Jake didn't like to draw comparisons because if that were true that would mean Jake was an asshole, too. "Are you disappointed?"

"Oh, stop. Why would I be disappointed? It was just a question. Revealing something personal about yourself doesn't make you weak, you know. It's not as if I'm going to hold what you tell me against you. You can be such a bear. Would you like a Cheese Nibble? You seem peckish."

"Peckish?"

"Yeah, you know…hungry and grouchy?"

He suppressed an unwelcome grin. That girl had a way of worming her way beneath his skin in the most beguiling way. "I don't eat Cheese Nibbles. Too full of preservatives."

She exhaled an annoyed breath. "Are you always so rigid? I noticed you line your shoes up at the edge of the bed. Military training, I assume?"

"Affirmative."

"Which branch?"

"Army."

"Ohh, army strong. Yeah, I think that fits you. You seem hewn from granite. I mean your physique is pretty impressive. Now, mind you, I hang out with scientists all day and although I'm loath to perpetuate a stereotype, where there's smoke there's fire. As in…not many of my peers were big on going to the gym. They were pretty soft in the muscle department."

Jake cut her a sidewise look, wildly and inappropriately curious about her personal life. "So…scientists are your type? You like the brainy guys?"

"I like—" she bit her lip as if embarrassed and peeped at him "—guys like you. Smart *and* underwear model material." Her cheeks pinked and she averted her stare as if she just couldn't handle watching his reaction to her admission. What did she think he was going to do? Laugh? Mock her? Something told him that maybe that had happened to her in the past and a growl threatened to erupt from his lips. She continued, keeping her gaze trained out the window at the passing scenery. "But I'm not exactly the kind of girl who gets noticed by guys like you. I mean, it's okay. I'm not crying over it or anything but high school was rough. Smart girls aren't what's considered hot with teenage boys."

"Then they were not only stupid but blind, too," he muttered before he could stop his unruly mouth. He tightened his lips but it was too late. He caught the quick look Kat shot him and he shrugged. "Listen, teenage boys are stupid. I should know, I was one. Kat, you've got nothing to be ashamed of in the looks department, okay?"

A slow, shy but utterly delighted smile curved her

lips and something gripped his insides with an iron claw. "You mean it? Wait, of course you do. You're not the kind of guy who would blithely hand out compliments just to feed someone's ego."

"I'm not?" he asked, amused.

"No, not at all."

"You think you have me figured out?"

"Not completely figured out, but definitely, mildly figured out. You're the kind of guy who would never say the words *I Love You* unless you meant them because you believe in the power of the words. You would never lie to someone just to spare them the pain of the truth. You are the kind of guy who believes in ripping the bandage quickly, rather than pulling it slowly. And, you would do anything for someone you cared about."

He sat in shock. How'd she manage to glean all that from their short acquaintance? It was spooky. Jake forced a small shrug. "Maybe. Or maybe not. Maybe I'm nothing like you think."

"You didn't have to drive me. You could've forced me to fly. What do you care about my phobia? Or the fact that I'm allergic to anesthesia? It wasn't your problem. That single action told me that you were the kind of guy who cares about people."

Jake didn't want her romanticizing his actions. That could only lead to heartache on her end when he ultimately disappointed her. As much as he hated to do it, he had to pop a hole in her theory. "I'm flattered but before you go too far, my concern was for the mission.

My mission is to secure you safely to Washington. I can't have your health jeopardized by anything I can prevent, so a road trip was necessary."

She smiled as if she knew a secret and it was that look that scared him more than staring down the barrel of a gun—because whatever she knew, it was probably accurate. "Kat, I don't want you to get the wrong idea. Okay?" he prompted gently.

"I'm not," she assured him, but Jake still wasn't sure if he was getting his point across. In the end, he decided to drop it. Maybe she was right. He was peckish. "Hand me a Cheese Nibble," he said, relenting. As he chewed, he wondered how it was that this slip of a scientist had begun twisting him in knots in record time when he'd faced far greater threats in the past. One thing Kat was right about…her life was never going to be the same nor was she likely going to be able to continue her research into a cure for Alzheimer's. That more than anything made his gut churn. And he wasn't looking forward to the moment when she learned her dreams of creating a cure would have to be shelved.

Nope…not looking forward to that at all.

"Are we almost there?" she asked, tossing back a few nibbles. "I have to pee again. Small bladder. Bane of my existence."

"Yeah," he answered. "Another half hour."

She groaned but otherwise fell silent and Jake was glad. He needed to regroup. Get it together, he told himself. Easier said than done.

* * *

When Kat found herself humming, she nearly barked a short laugh. There was nothing remotely cheery about her current situation and yet she felt strangely content to be sitting in the passenger seat next to Jake, driving to who knows where to evade who knows who so as not to be kidnapped and forced to create a weapon of mass destruction. When she broke it down, her silly humming was ludicrous. But she liked spending time with Jake. Were all government agents as handsome as he was? She was mooning over her captor. She pursed her lips. How did she feel about that? She considered herself a relatively logical person but the way she felt about Jake was completely irrational. And possibly dangerous. A subtle thrill curled itself around her spine and she shuddered. How many times had she wished something exciting would happen to her? Too many to count. Her uncle had warned her to be careful what she wished for.

Her hormones were playing badminton with her brain, because she was having estrogen-soaked fantasies that featured Jake Isaacs in all his (naked) glory. Of course, she had to fill in the blanks because she hadn't actually seen Jake in his birthday suit and, to be honest, she didn't have all that many other naked men experiences to help her imagination along but male anatomy was basically the same, right?

She certainly didn't want to die a virgin. *Bigger problems,* she reminded herself dryly, but she swatted that thought away. Kat had lived her entire life being a certain way and now circumstances had come along to challenge that in a big way. She couldn't help but wonder if she'd been putting the emphasis on all the wrong things. Not that her research wasn't important— goodness gracious, no—but maybe she should've spent a little less time in the lab and more interacting with real people. Monkeys are no substitute for humans. And now she was woefully undereducated in the ways of how to successfully flirt and engage in coy banter with the opposite sex. Her one attempt at seduction had blown up in her face, leaving her embarrassed and feeling pathetic but she wasn't going to give up, because she wanted Jake and she wanted him bad.

"How many women have you slept with?" she blurted out, and Jake did a quick double take.

"What? Why?" he asked.

"Don't be shy. Just tell me. I promise not to judge you. Besides, with the whole double standard thing it's impossible for men to come off as promiscuous no matter how many sexual partners they've had."

"I'm not promiscuous."

She smiled with relief. "Oh, that's good to know. But you've had enough experience to know what you're doing, right?" Smooth. Real smooth. "I mean, making love doesn't always come naturally, right? You have to learn your thing and your *moves*. I read somewhere that you're only as good in bed as your last lover." Which meant, since she'd never had a lover, she technically stunk. "Never mind. Just making conversation," she finished, her cheeks heating. "Feel free to pretend that I never said anything."

Jake paused as if he was going to remind her that they shouldn't talk about such personal topics, but he surprised her with an answer. "I've slept with five women in my lifetime."

"Only five?"

He cracked a smile that was plainly adorable and possibly made her ovaries quiver as he said, "Yeah, only five. Is that a good thing or a bad thing?"

"I wouldn't know. I've—" *Don't say it!* If she admitted she was a virgin he might get weird about knocking boots and she'd already decided that Jake was the one she wanted to initiate her into official womanhood. "Not having been with many people myself," she finished with a short smile. "But I am surprised for the aforementioned reasons."

He nodded in understanding, leaning his elbow against the door to rest his head against his fingertips. He looked cool like James Dean and Marlon Brando—*A Streetcar Named Desire* Brando, not *The Godfather* Brando—and Kat decided she had to know what it was like to be pressed up against a man like Jake as her co-pilot, particularly if she were on a collision course with danger. "I shouldn't be talking about stuff like this but, what the hell, the road is long and the drive boring. I don't sleep around because I find one-night stands unsatisfying. I need some kind of emotional connection necessary to fully enjoy a sexual encounter."

Did he just blush a little? Yes. He did and it was awesome. Kat smiled. "I think that's cool. I know some guys are pretty cavalier about their encounters."

"Yeah, just not my style. Plus, after I broke up with my girlfriend, I wasn't much interested in seeing anyone socially."

"Did she break your heart?" Kat asked, curious.

"Yeah, well, I think we did plenty of damage to one another. It was probably even. But we both decided we were better off without the other."

"Did you cheat on her?"

"No."

Why that mattered to Kat, she wasn't sure but when he answered, she felt the tension she wasn't even aware she was holding on to leave her shoulders. "So what went wrong?"

He shrugged. "Who knows. Probably just came down to the fact that we were going in separate directions and neither wanted to compromise."

"Do you regret breaking up?"

"If you're asking if I wish we were still together, the answer is no. If you're asking if I regret how I handled myself within the relationship, then yes. How about you?" he asked, turning the conversation back to her. "What kind of skeletons are dancing in your closet?"

Sadly…none. She didn't have any old boyfriends to lament. Time to change the subject. "Are we close? Not to ruin this awesome moment between us, but my bladder is really going to spring a leak if you know what I mean."

He laughed and didn't seem to notice that she'd completely avoided answering. "Yeah, two minutes and we're there. Can you hold your water until then?"

She nodded in relief but she was more relieved that she didn't need to make up war stories about the boyfriends she'd never had.

Really? First-world problems, she said to herself with an eye roll.

What could she say? It was the truth—a pathetic truth—but truth nonetheless.

Chapter 9

"Assuming it does what you say it does…I imagine we'd be interested in paying top dollar," the man across the table said, fingers toying with the straw wrapper from his straw but his eyes were deadly focused. "But then, how do we know it even works? What you're promising is a pretty tall order. The first of its kind."

"I have someone on the inside of Tessara Pharm who's been keeping tabs on the various experiments."

"And what is this Tessara Pharm?"

"A research lab and facility with its fingers in many pies. They manufacture a number of classified drugs the government uses that are not available to the private sector. There was a scuffle a while back about one of the founders but that's all been taken care of and they're back in business. Thankfully, only upper management was aware of this bump in the road. The busy bees in the lab kept on doing their work, productive as ever and one particular bee was very industrious, creating the drug that I've been explaining to you."

"How does Tessara get around the FDA with their government projects?"

He graced the man with a patronizing look. "Really? The FDA? Easily bought if you know the right people. You and I both know that there are certain factions within the FDA who have been willing to look the other way if the right amount of money has crossed palms."

"At times, yes, but those types of deals are shaky at best. Eventually, someone talks and rolls over. Such a potential scandal is not in our best interests."

At the man's open discomfort, he swallowed his irritation and said in a conciliatory tone, "I understand your concern. Your buyer certainly doesn't want to be tied to anything that might go sour. I can guarantee that won't happen."

"How?"

"Because this drug was a mistake and deemed a total failure. In fact, the scientist who created it was about to scrap the samples. I was able to procure a very limited quantity and field-test it myself."

At that the man, known only as Mr. Blue, leaned forward with interest. "I want to see it for myself."

"As I said, the sample was limited and also, unfortunately, unstable. Our field test wasn't entirely successful but we feel very confident that once we have possession of the scientist, she will be able to work out the kinks in the formula."

"Why do you need the scientist? If you could get the samples, why not her research notes? Surely, you have scientists in your employ who can follow a road map someone else had drawn?"

"Of course we do," he said, shifting with mild embarrassment. "But they can't make heads or tails of her notes. Apparently, she wrote in some kind of code that only she understands."

"Why would she do that?" he asked.

"Hell if I know," he grumbled, freshly annoyed at being made to look foolish. It wasn't often that he found himself in that position and he didn't like it. If he hadn't needed that scientist, he would've put a bullet in her head for good measure. "But you needn't worry. We have the scientist in our possession and she will perfect her formula."

Mr. Blue scowled. "You're asking my client to pay millions for a faulty formula? If this is a joke, I find it in entirely bad taste."

"I wouldn't dream of playing you false, Mr. Blue. Let me show you," he said, pulling his cell phone from his pocket and going to the video files. He pressed play and handed it to the man. The man's expression went from annoyed to curious and then shock. He smiled as Mr. Blue returned the phone. "Dr. Odgers had limited opportunity to truly field-test the formula because her research was limited to the monkey test subjects. We were able to procure *human* subjects to test the sample. As you can see…the results are quite promising."

"Yes," Mr. Blue agreed, rubbing his chin in thought. "Until his eyes rolled into his head and he fell over. Is he dead?"

"No, but the poor bastard will not be doing any mental calisthenics anytime soon."

"Brain dead?"

"Regrettably."

"Well, that's no good. The allure of the drug is the clean nature of its ability to erase memory."

"I agree, which is why we are procuring the scientist and she will fix that little problem."

"And what if she can't?"

"She will."

"Your confidence borders on arrogance but I cannot take those assurances to the bank. We're talking a lot of money. We will not pay for a faulty drug."

"And I would never presume to ask you to. However, there's a certain level of risk involved for me."

"Yes, I would assume so. What's your interest in doing this?"

"Isn't it obvious?"

"Money?"

"Of course," he answered coolly but that was only the surface answer. He couldn't explain the rush he got from selling government secrets. He'd been doing it for years under the radar—nothing that could be traced back to him, of course—and those secrets had nicely lined his bank account but the game had turned stale. Until MCX-209. He'd always speculated that the newest hot ticket in espionage and terrorism would be found in technological and pharmaceutical advances, which is why he'd cleverly made a friend within Tessara Pharm who funneled information to him on the current experiments with promise or interest. And that one decision was about to pay off in dividends beyond his wildest dreams. But now he had to deal with the unpleasant aspect of backdoor deals and Mr. Blue wasn't going to like what he had to say so he might as well get it over with. "I should warn you that you are not the only interested buyer," he said, throwing it out there without apology.

Mr. Blue's stare narrowed. "This was not an exclusive offer?"

"I apologize for the misunderstanding but no. Whoever ponies up the most cash—the fastest—will get the formula. I am effectively ruining my career for this deal. Surely, you can understand my need to get the most bang for my buck."

"Send me the video and I will show my people," he growled, clearly unhappy. "We will be in touch."

"Of course," he said, nodding. "I await your call."

Mr. Blue—a dangerous man in an expensive suit— melted into the throng of people clustered around the outdoor patio dining area and disappeared.

He chuckled and tucked his phone back into his suit pocket for safekeeping. Now, all he needed was that damn scientist. If Jake Isaacs didn't deliver, he'd just have to find someone else who would.

Failure wasn't an option.

But death certainly was.

Jake found Nathan's place without too many wrong turns and, while it wasn't much to look at, Jake appreciated its strategic advantages. He had a clear vantage point from every direction and there was little fear of anyone sneaking up on them, which Jake found a plus. Added to the fact that no one knew where they were, was another advantage.

Kat surveyed the expansive view of the Sierra Nevada mountain range and said, "Your brother have a thing against neighbors?"

"He likes his privacy," Jake answered, opening the front door and motioning for her to follow. After a quick perimeter search, Jake returned to the car and retrieved their gear as well as what they had left in food, which wasn't much.

"Check the cupboards and see if there's anything edible around while I look for batteries," he instructed, going straight for the drawers. Rifling through them, he found a stash of batteries and began putting fresh ones into the lamps. At her questioning look, he explained, "No power. My brother didn't want anything that might compromise his position, if the need ever arose."

"Geesh, was he preparing for the apocalypse?" she asked, opening a cupboard to reveal a cache of MREs.

She grimaced at the realization that she was looking at their dinner. "So, no power…what about the toilets? There are toilets, right?"

"Of course, but they're compost toilets."

"I know what that is in theory but I've never actually used one," she admitted, secretly hating the idea of using anything aside from a regular commode for her business. "Is it complicated?"

"Not at all. It's all contained. Go see for yourself. It looks just like a regular toilet, except solids go in one place and liquids go in another."

She groaned. "Why can't it just be a regular toilet like everyone else in the world uses?" she asked, succumbing to a moment of whining.

"What happened to the woman who wanted to limit her footprint? Compost toilets are very green."

"They're very gross," she argued.

"Well, you could squat behind a bush, I suppose," Jake said, shrugging, but added as if to soften his suggestion, "We won't be here long. Chances are we'll be gone in a day or two."

She nodded and grabbed a lamp. "Well, I guess I'd better get acquainted with this *green* technology because I have to pee. Are there any instructions?"

"I could show you or you could read the diagram taped to the wall."

"I'll figure it out," Kat said with a grumble, not interested in talking about bathroom stuff with Jake. She was a genius for crying out loud. If she couldn't figure out how to work a toilet, she didn't deserve to call herself a scientist.

"In the meantime, I'll fire up some dinners. Any preference?" he called out, and she responded by slamming the bathroom door. Preference was an illusion when it came to MRE dining. She'd give anything for her processed macaroni and cheese.

Kat placed the lamp on the rudimentary vanity and stared at the simple toilet that looked as if it belonged in an old folk's home and sighed with resignation as her bladder protested the holdup. After a quick read-through of the instructions, she did her business and successfully used the compost toilet. Not so bad, she thought. But there was no way she was giving up her commode. No way. She'd give up plastic bags and if she ever had kids, she'd promise to use cloth diapers but she was *not* going to change to a composting toilet.

"See that wasn't so bad, was it?" Jake teased, sliding her MRE of spaghetti and meatballs across the counter toward her.

Kat stopped the plate of Frankenfood and graced Jake with a look that said he was crazy. "Wait until you have to empty the liquid reservoir...that ought to be fun."

"I'm sure I've dealt with far worse in the past," he assured her, shoveling a bite into his mouth as if he were enjoying a plate of the finest cuisine. He gestured to her plate. "Eat up. This stuff doesn't taste good cold."

"It doesn't taste good hot, either," she quipped, but

scooped a mouthful because she was starving. She had the metabolism of a hummingbird and she needed food. "Okay, this one isn't as bad as the last one I ate but I wouldn't choose to eat this."

"Why not?" Jake asked, frowning. "It's perfect fuel."

"Food is not just fuel. Food is a sensory orchestra."

"If you say so."

"Haven't you ever experienced food that is so good, it's like a song in your mouth?"

"No."

"You haven't lived, then," Kat decided, taking another bite and pretending it was far better than it was. "My uncle was an amazing cook. When he got stuck with me, he'd finally been accepted into Cordon Bleu in San Francisco but he knew he couldn't complete the course work with a kid waiting for him at home, so he declined the invitation. But he never stopped trying to be the best he could be in the kitchen. He could make anything taste good. His one regret was that he couldn't shake my preference for processed macaroni and cheese. He tried so hard, too. Once, he made an organic baked macaroni and cheese and it was pretty good but it was missing that certain something. But I loved him for trying." She tried to keep the wistfulness from her voice but she couldn't help it. Talking about her uncle was always a trigger for the waterworks. She straightened and poked at her noodles. "Anyway, my uncle introduced me to culinary masterpieces I never would've thought to try on my own."

"Such as?"

"Rack of lamb, shrimp scampi, crab fettuccini, Italian soup, just to name a few."

Jake fell silent for a moment, then said, "Meals around my place weren't always the standard fare. We were lucky to get a bowl of stale cereal with powdered milk. My old man would drink away his paycheck, which wouldn't leave my mom with much to buy groceries with. The most wholesome meals we ate were at school. Thank God for subsidized food programs, otherwise we might've starved. I grew up to realize that food was simply fuel. Without it, your body stops functioning."

Jake's admission pulled at her heart. She imagined the little boy he might've been, hungry and bone-thin, and knew if her uncle had been in Jake's life, he would've stuffed him with all manner of good food just as he'd done to her. "Every child deserves a good childhood," Kat said softly. "I'm sorry yours was so bad. Do you have any happy memories at all?"

"Sure," he said, surprising her. "That's the thing about kids…no matter how bad the situation, they always manage to find a bright spot somewhere. Nathan and I used to go down to the creek during the summer and spend all day in the water. Our parents never cared where we went as long as we were out of their hair. Summers were better than winter because at least we could get away from them when it was hot. Winters were bleak. There was never enough wood for the fireplace, and it was too cold to go outside. Stuck inside with them was the worst." He shot her a quick look. "What were your parents like?"

"Adventurous," she answered with a smile. "And nothing like me. I used to wonder if I was switched at birth. They were so full of life. Hence, the skydiving in Brazil that killed them."

"Where were you when this happened?"

"I was in Brazil, too. I was staying with a babysitter while they went to fly through the air. We were supposed to go to dinner when they returned. I don't remember much after that. I think I blanked it out. Too painful. The next memory I have was being deposited with my uncle and crying a lot."

"Your uncle sounds like a good man to take in his orphaned niece."

"He was the best. He shelved everything in his life for me. I don't know how I could ever repay him for that. He didn't have to put his life on hold for me. Before that moment, he'd only ever seen me at a few Christmas dinners."

"At least you had someone to take you in," he said. "You could've ended up in foster care or worse, an orphanage."

"Oh, I know how lucky I was. That's why I owe such a debt of gratitude to him."

"I wish we'd had someone in our lives who would've been willing to take us in, not that my parents would've latched loose, but it would've been nice to know some-one out there cared."

She nodded. "Feeling alone is the worst feeling in the world."

He looked ready to agree, but then he must've re-alized he was sharing too much and pulled back, crumpling his trash and tossing it away in the trash compactor. "I'm going to do another perimeter search and then get our rooms situated. You good here?"

"Yeah, sure," she said, disappointed in how quickly he reverted to Roboman when faced with sharing some-thing personal. She pushed away her own tray of half-eaten food and sighed. How was she going to manage to get past that barrier if Jake didn't let anyone get close to him? She understood why he kept the wall up—you couldn't get hurt if you didn't let anyone in. She knew that tactic pretty well, actually. Her childhood may not have been as tragic as Jake's but her high school years were a blur of memories she was happy to leave be-hind. Suffice to say, Kat Odgers knew a thing or two about rejection.

She also knew how much it hurt to watch the world pass by from the sidelines.

And she had a feeling Jake knew, too.

Chapter 10

The place is secure, he told himself after his third perimeter search. At this point he was just tromping in circles in a lame attempt to avoid the real issue—the sleeping arrangements.

The minute he returned inside, Kat yawned and looked pointedly in his direction and he felt sweat pop along his hairline, though he did his best to appear as if he wasn't feeling all edgy and twitchy like a damn meth addict.

"I'm really tired," Kat said, rising. "Can you show me which room is going to be mine?"

"You're sleeping with me," he blurted out with little grace or forethought. What the hell was wrong with him? He hadn't meant to announce it with so little preparation. God, he probably sounded like a bully. He cleared his throat and tried again, saying, "What I mean to say is, it's safer if we stick together. With circumstances being the way they are, I would feel more secure if there wasn't a wall separating us."

Her cheeks pinked but she nodded vigorously. "Of course! That's a very sound decision and I completely agree. I was going to suggest it but I didn't want to seem as if I were just some silly woman eager to jump into bed with you. Because that's not the case, you know."

"Of course not," he said gruffly. "This is strictly a safety precaution."

"Yes. And I appreciate you making the sacrifice for me. I know I can be a bed hog."

"You're not a bed hog. If anyone is making a sacrifice, it's you. I tend to kick the covers off."

"I noticed that but it's not a terrible offense. I can live with it." She added hastily, "In the short term."

He jerked a nod, glad that was done, but his chest felt incredibly tight, as if he was being used as a footstool for an elephant. He couldn't stand the idea of sleeping apart but the knowledge that they were going to share a bed again filled him with tension. There was no winning this war with himself, he realized and let it go. No sense in dwelling. "Let's turn in, then," he suggested, going to shut off the lamps and double-check the locks before they headed to the master bedroom. He rummaged through his bag and found the T-shirt he'd given her to borrow the previous night and tossed it to her.

She accepted it with a small smile. "It's the best I can do at the moment," Jake said.

"Thank you. I'm going to change," she announced, then added, "Would you mind terribly if you shut off the lights before I come back out?"

"Of course," he said, happy to oblige her modesty and thankful for her foresight. He didn't know how he would handle seeing her so scantily dressed again. He was holding tightly to the reins of his control and just the memory of her sweet body caused his hands to tremble with the need to touch. He pulled his shirt free and folded it neatly, followed by his jeans. As always he lined his boots up beside the bed. Satisfied, he climbed into the double bed and clicked off the lights.

He squeezed his eyes shut so as not to catch even the tiniest glimpse of Kat's body and only opened them when he felt the mattress give under her slight weight as the covers went over her. Tense silence filled the small room when they both realized the bed was entirely too small to avoid touching one another. "I'm sorry if I'm crowding you," he said.

"You're not," she said in a small voice. "I feel…safe."

Her admission caused a warmth to spread across his body. He liked knowing that he was the one who made her feel that way. "Good," he said, allowing a tiny smile. Minute by minute he slowly relaxed until when he was turning on his side, and he accidentally brushed flesh.

Flesh that should've been covered by his T-shirt.

"Kat…what are you wearing?"

Her tremulous answer nearly stopped his heart. "Nothing."

And Jake knew they were both in trouble.

Would he reject her? Kat's heart galloped like a wild horse inside her chest as she held her breath, desperately hoping he wouldn't scoff at her attempt at seduction, though she had to admit, it was a little on the pathetic side. When the heavy silence dragged on, Kat started talking as if her life depended on it.

"I know how this looks," she began hurriedly. "I'm throwing myself at you in some lame attempt at seduction and I wish I could deny it but it's true. I don't know the first thing about being sexy or coy, or how to get a guy to look at me in a romantic way, but the truth of the matter is, there's a good chance I might die soon and I refuse to die without knowing what it's like to be held and kissed by a man like you."

"Kat—"

"No, let me say this while I still have the courage," she interrupted, not willing to be shut down, not yet. "Jake…I want to know what I've been missing all these years. Let me tell you about my high school years. They were short and painful. I graduated early so I could get away from all the mean bullies who made my life miserable. I never got asked to the prom and I never got the dubious pleasure of suffering through awkward dates and fumbling backseat make-out sessions. You know what I was doing my teenage years? Studying. I was obsessed with graduating early because somehow I thought college would be better and it was, to a point. But I still missed out on some key college experiences."

"Such as?" he asked, but his voice sounded strangely tight.

"Well, just by stereotypical standards, I never got the chance to question my sexuality. What if I like girls? I never got to kiss a girl. For that matter, I didn't get to kiss that many boys, either, and the ones I kissed weren't the hunky jocks. They were science nerds, like me. And contrary to that movie, *Revenge of the Nerds,* nerds are not better at it just because they fantasize more." She grimaced at the memory of the slobberfest, clumsy tongue tangling that had occurred with her Physics lab partner. *Ugh. What a mistake that had been.* "The point is, I've missed out on a lot and I don't want to go to my grave wishing I'd grabbed an opportunity when I still had a chance." She leaned over to Jake and put her hand tentatively on his chest. She thrilled at the scant amount of chest hair she found beneath her fingertips. "Please, Jake…I need this."

His fingers closed over hers and for a distressing moment she thought for sure he was going to gently remove her hand from his chest but instead he said softly, "Those boys were fools if they couldn't see what a beautiful woman you are."

Her breath hitched and foolish tears flooded her eyes. Why did it mean so much to hear him say that to her? She desperately wanted to believe that he spoke from his heart, but she was afraid he was only being polite. "You don't have to say that. I've never been beautiful in my life and I've made peace with my looks."

"You know I wouldn't say something I didn't believe," he reminded her in a sultry whisper that made her toes curl. "Come here."

She felt woozy but she leaned forward and nearly swooned when his soft lips met hers. "I don't really know what I'm doing," she admitted, nervousness setting in. This must be what performance anxiety felt like. "Perhaps you could give me some tips…"

"Kat, stop thinking so much," Jake said with a growl against her lips. "And for God's sake, stop talking."

"Easier said than d—" Kat gasped as suddenly Jake's hand took possession of her bare breast, shocking her into silence and catapulting her senses into pure overdrive. Jake took full advantage of her surprised silence and claimed her lips again, only this time, he demanded full participation, dipping his tongue inside her mouth while kneading her breast and causing her to whimper as tendrils of something wondrous began seeking out and electrifying her every erogenous zone.

"Oh!" she cried, wanting more of whatever this amazing feeling was. This was arousal, she realized dizzily. That crazy, almost-drunk feeling that people talked about in hushed whispers—that thing that toppled kingdoms and drove people to madness—*yes!* Oh, she liked it. No, she loved it! Female empowerment filled her veins and took control of her limbs as she wrapped her arms around Jake and pressed herself more closely against his hard, firm body. She gave herself fully to Jake's marauding kisses, delighted in the way her skin danced with sensation as he devoured her flesh as if starved. And just when she thought it couldn't become more fevered, more intense, Jake's mouth descended on her—goodness gracious, she couldn't even say the word!—but who needed words, anyway? His tongue! Plunging and tasting—kissing in the deepest, most sensual way—made her gulp the night air with desperate heaving breaths as an embarrassingly animalistic moan was ripped from her throat.

"Jake!" she cried, stiffening against the onslaught of beautiful glory that sang from her loins. This was heaven! Why had she waited so long? She crashed back to earth to a rushing in her ears and she realized dimly it was the blood screaming through her veins as her heart worked double-time.

That was awesome.

And she wanted to do it again.

Jake was hard as a stone but he managed to pull back before he took Kat without thought. His brain wasn't entirely functioning properly. He knew he shouldn't have done it but he was helpless to stop once he heard Kat's impassioned plea. Well, that and the fact that she was naked pretty much destroyed every defense he had.

But he had a sense she was a virgin and he couldn't take that from her…not like this. She deserved far better for her first time than a desperate poke from a virtual stranger. Except when he thought of someone else taking her virginity, he wanted to punch something. If he'd been thinking clearly, that one irrational feeling would've been the biggest red flag but he was nowhere near thinking clearly. All he wanted was to feel Kat beneath him. Her scent was on his mouth, chasing away the last vestige of rationality available to him and he was driven by a primal need to possess.

But somewhere, deep inside, a voice cautioned and he heard its dim call. He slowed his kisses but couldn't quite stop completely as he framed her face with his hands to ask, "Kat, are you sure? Tell me to stop and I will."

"Don't you dare stop! I've waited too long for something this wonderful to happen to me," she said in a breathy whisper. "I want this. I want this more than you can possibly know."

"You're a virgin, aren't you?" he asked, almost afraid to know the answer.

She hesitated before replying. "Yes," she admitted, and he heard the anxiety in her voice. "You're not going to hold that against me are you?"

"God, no. But—"

"But nothing. I'm not stupid. I know what I'm doing. Um, well, I know what I'm doing, per se, but I don't really *know* what I'm doing, you know?"

He laughed at that. "Yes, I get it. I just want you to

be sure. I don't want you to regret giving me something so precious."

He heard her inhale and worried he might've said something wrong but when she sealed her mouth to his, that fleeting moment of rational thought fled and within moments they were too wrapped up in each other to question whether their actions were prudent.

But when the moment occurred, Jake took care to enter her slowly, listening for the slightest indication of pain or distress, but aside from the smallest gasp, Kat simply wrapped her legs around his torso and pulled him deeper still. "Kat...wait," he said between gritted teeth, desperately trying not to hurt her but she had other plans.

"It's just a thin sheath of skin. I'm not made of China. I promise I won't break," she said, but he could tell she wasn't enjoying this part. He'd never been with a virgin before and the pressure to make it pleasurable was nearly overwhelming until he felt the flutter light touch of her fingertips, smoothing away the tension in his forehead. "It's okay," she whispered, kissing him softly. "I promise."

"I'm supposed to be the one reassuring you," he said, returning the kiss and thrusting his hips gently. The building pressure in his loins signaled an impending end before they'd truly begun. He groaned, needing to last longer than a few thrusts. "I...need to think of baseball, I think," he said.

"Baseball? That's an odd turn-on," she said, laughing.

"It's not a turn-on. I hate baseball."

"Oh, wait…what?"

"Sweet Kat…I'm trying to last but I'm really close to blowing," he admitted, his eyes nearly crossing from the insane pressure. "God, I promise I'm usually able to last much longer. This is really embarrassing."

She giggled and kissed him. "I find that incredibly sexy. And sweet. If you promise we can try this again… you can do your thing."

"Negotiating?" Impressive. And damn hot. He kissed her hard. "Deal."

He may have just made a deal with the devil but at the moment, he didn't care.

All that mattered was the moment.

All that mattered was Kat.

Chapter 11

Kat stared up at the ceiling, listening to Jake's labored breathing and she felt the unmistakably giddy feeling of infatuation setting in. She'd resigned herself to the knowledge that her first time would likely suck. That it likely would occur with someone far less sexy or virile as Jake Isaacs. Boy, was she glad she'd been way off. She turned to face Jake, happy as a clam, but her silly smile faded when she saw his somber expression. "What's wrong?" she asked. "Did I do something wrong? Was I that bad? I'm a fast learner. If you give me some tips—"

"It's not that," he cut in. "You were…*perfect*." Even though he bit out the word with some reluctance, Kat warmed with delicious pleasure. Jake put his laced hands over his eyes and exhaled as if the weight of the world had just landed on his shoulders. "Kat…I shouldn't have—"

"Don't say it." Now it was her turn to interrupt. "Don't you go saying that you regret what happened between us because that will ruin all the wonderful feelings I have right now. I know all of the ethical reasons and professional reasons why you might think you did something wrong but I'm telling you, don't waste your energy on those feelings. I wanted this. I set out to seduce you." At his raised brow, she nodded vigorously, owning every syllable. "That's right. I did. I knew I wanted you to be my first. Probably from the moment I saw you. Subconsciously, of course. And I don't feel the least bit troubled by it."

"Kat, you don't understand…I've never lost control of myself like this. I've never ignored my training because of a woman. Any woman. Except you."

"Okay, I'm not sure if I should be flattered or insulted."

"Definitely flattered," he said. "But I've compromised myself and the mission by giving in to your *seduction*."

"How have you compromised the mission?"

"No personal ties. I'm not supposed to feel anything for the targets."

"Well, you're not a robot. You're a human being. It's only natural that you would feel *something* for another person. Besides, this is an extreme situation. Like in

Speed, when Sandra Bullock and Keanu Reeves fall in love after the bus incident. Extreme emotion can mimic the feelings of infatuation. I should know. Right now, I'm feeling really infatuated with you. Especially with that thing you did with your tongue." She blushed but held his gaze. "I mean, what woman wouldn't? That was pretty spectacular."

The corners of his mouth twitched. "But the other part was only so-so, right?"

"Well, to be fair, it was my first time. I suspect it gets better, right?"

"With the right partner, yes."

She read between the lines and didn't like the message. "Are you saying that was a one-and-done as they say? You promised we could do it again," she reminded with a frown. "Aren't you a man of your word?"

"Kat! Come on, cut me some damn slack. I'm trying to do the right thing here."

"And I don't want you to do the right thing," she snapped, irritated. "I want you to show me how great sex can be. I'm not asking you to marry me. I just want to know what it's like to lose myself in another human being before I die. Is that so much to ask?"

"Stop talking about dying. I'm not going to let anything happen to you, you goose."

"Well, I don't know that and you can't promise me that. So, I would rather grab hold of my opportunities as I find them."

"Are you saying you would've had sex with anyone handy during this ordeal?" he asked, offended at the idea.

"Now you're just being ridiculous."

He sighed. Was it bad that she wanted to jump his bones again right this second? She bit her lip. Men needed a recovery period, according to her research. "Do you think you'll be sufficiently recovered by morning? I'd like to squeeze in another romp before we have to go back on the run. Or we could try it in the car! I'm open to experimenting. I have a lot of time to make up for."

Jake groaned and then laughed as if she were the strangest woman he'd ever come across.

"I can't believe how blithely you're talking about sex for someone who was only just introduced to it."

"Well, like I said, I've lost out on a lot and I think I have a pretty active interest in sex now that I've been given a taste. I might even be insatiable. Or maybe this is normal? I don't know. What do you think?"

"I think I have no idea how to answer that," he said. "A part of me is in shock that we're talking about it at all."

"Yeah, it's probably a strange conversation to have with someone, particularly someone you don't know very well aside from carnally. Tell me something about yourself that no one else would know."

Jake did a double take. "What do you mean?"

"Lovers should know private details about one another. Maybe if we share information, it will make things less awkward between us."

Jake paused and for a moment, but he finally said, "When I was a kid, I was afraid of clowns."

"Isn't every kid?" she teased lightly, and he chuckled. Kat wanted to know everything about Jake and hungered for every morsel of information tossed her way. Was this normal? This desire to climb in to someone's life and attach yourself to it in some way? She knew the answer—it wasn't. But there was something about Jake that felt right in every way, even before they'd been intimate, and if she weren't so drunk on the afterglow of their lovemaking, she might've paused to question herself. But she didn't want to question or examine the how or why. She only wanted to feel. "I am allergic to cats."

"Cats and anesthesia. Check. Anything else I should know?"

A playful smile curved her lips. *I might be becoming addicted to you.* "No. Not that I'm aware but that's half the problem with allergens…sometimes you don't know about them until you're puffing up and going into anaphylactic shock."

"Good point."

Kat yawned and decided it was time to catch some shut-eye. She was wondrously drowsy all of a sudden. "Sex is a good workout. And to think I've been wasting all that time on the treadmill when I could've been doing this. Good night, Jake."

"Good night, Kat," he said, startling her when he

pulled her to him. She smiled and snuggled against him. This was perfect, she thought as she drifted to sleep with Jake's arms curled around her. Absolutely perfect, she thought with a happy sigh. Except for the impending death part—that part she could do without.

Dumb-ass rookie mistake, Jake berated himself as he listened to Kat's soft, even breathing. But he couldn't deny that Kat fit quite nicely up against him. Everything about her called to him with a siren's song that he couldn't fathom but ultimately couldn't resist, either. What was he doing? Losing his edge. How was this possible? Not a clue. But what was the point of denying that he was strangely—recklessly—attracted to Kat? How was it possible that she got prettier each time he looked at her? And now that he'd taken her cherry? He suppressed an all-over shudder of awareness and tightened his hold on her. He'd never felt so damn possessive in his life. He'd always thought the whole *primal urge* thing was a crock of shit. People who couldn't control themselves were simply weak. It was a hard pill to swallow that he'd suddenly fallen into that category.

But he'd do it again. In a heartbeat. Feeling Kat beneath him, swallowing her cries in his mouth, being the first man to know her carnally…it wound his clock in the worst way. Had he ever in his life been so reckless with a woman? He searched his memory and came up empty. In fact, a different memory came up that was the exact opposite.

"Relationships slow you down, make you vulnerable," Nathan had advised him, shortly before he'd split for good. The two had been down at the creek, staying out as long as possible to avoid running into their father, who was likely drunker than hell and ready for a fight. Nathan, at seventeen, was always a good target. Jake had asked why Nathan had broken up with his girlfriend, Darla. Little had Jake known then that Nathan had been cutting ties so he could bail without attachments. *"Besides, there's no sense in sticking to one when there's plenty others out there to take their place."*

"I thought you liked Darla," Jake said. *"She seemed pretty cool and she's hot."*

"Yeah, well, I ain't looking to find a wife. There ain't a girl out there smart enough to find a way to put a ring on this finger."

"It might be nice to have someone who's always on your side, you know?"

"There ain't no one out there like that. Given the right circumstances, everyone is willing to stab you in the back if you let them."

Jake didn't want to believe that. He knew his parents had a rotten marriage—likely because his mom and dad were both rotten people—but surely not everyone was like that.

"Are you saying that you'd stab me in the back?" Jake asked Nathan.

"Brothers are different."

Relief flooded Jake's chest. His brother was all he

had in this world. "Well, I kinda like Lily Frazier. I was thinking of asking her out. What do you think?"

"That the redhead?" *Nathan asked, and Jake nodded.* "She's cute enough, I guess. You know you can't bring her around Mom and Dad, right?"

"Hell, yeah," *Jake answered with a snort.* "I ain't dumb."

"Good. Just checking. If you like her, go for it. Have fun but don't get attached. When you get attached...they can be used against you as a weakness. You get me? Especially if Mom and Dad find out."

Jake nodded at the solid advice. "I'll keep it on the down low."

"Good." *Nathan closed his eyes, swinging his feet off the rock they were lying on, his toes skimming the water. Then he sighed.* "I guess we better head back."

"Yeah, I guess. Think he's passed out yet?"

"Let's hope," *Nathan replied grimly.* "Go around the back and enter through the kitchen. Chances are he's passed out in his recliner by now with Mom sacked out in her bed."

"Yeah...hopefully."

But luck hadn't been on their side. In fact, their old man had been waiting for them both. Jake still had a scar on his back from where the belt hook had dug into his skin and ripped it wide-open. Nathan's scars went even deeper. Jake wondered if Nathan's girl, Jaci, knew half the crap that had gone down in their childhood. No child should have to live through what Nathan and Jake had.

And just as one memory faded, another intruded.

"You think you're so smart," his father had sneered to Jake one night, so drunk his words slurred. Their mother was out and, although she was never much help, at least when she was around their father seemed to tone down his attacks. Nathan's theory was that the old man didn't want anyone who could testify against him in court if by chance one of his kids died from his "punishments."

Jake, eleven and still scrawny, was no match for his father, and the familiar tremble of fear had begun to quiver in his belly. "Get over here, boy. I'm gonna wipe that look clean off your stupid face," his father had demanded, but Jake had refused, knowing that to get within grabbing distance of his father would mean ending the night with possible broken bones. Sometimes their father seemed eaten by a rage that he could only assuage through violence. And for some reason, he delighted in taking out his rage on his boys. There'd been no mercy—ever.

That night Nathan had been gone. There'd been no one to protect him. And no one to hear his cries.

And when it was all over? No one to take him to the hospital.

Just the recollection of that night managed to cause sweat to slick his skin. Jake tried never to think of those memories. He buried them deep with the express intention of never giving them air. It'd been a long time since he'd thought of those days, but since Nathan had returned to his life, all sorts of buried pain had started to resurface. And now on top of that, he had Kat to contend with. As his commanding officer in the army, Colonel Ralph Rangdon, used to tell his troops when they went on leave, "Men, think with your heads—not your peckers!"

Good advice then, good advice now.

And yet…unlike then, today he'd completely done the opposite.

What was he going to do? He supposed he'd have to get it figured out before someone got hurt—someone like Kat.

Chapter 12

Kat awoke to an empty bed—not the reception she was hoping for after their intimate night together—but she wasn't entirely surprised, either. While she was happy as a clam throwing caution to the wind, Jake had clearly been eaten up by their lack of control. Kat had never met a more wound-up man with control issues than Jake. Was it weird that in spite of this, she found him wildly alluring?

She climbed from the bed, wincing at the inevitable soreness in private places as well as within muscles that had never previously been exercised, and padded from the bedroom to find Jake doing push-ups in the living room. From the sweat glistening on his back, Kat surmised he'd been out here for a while.

Hello, excellent male specimen. She leaned against the door frame, waiting for him to finish and enjoying the show. Every muscle stood out in relief against his bronzed skin and she envisioned with startling clarity how she'd love to give him a tongue bath. Instead, she said from the doorway, "I know I'm new to this but I was surprised to wake up alone this morning. Is everything okay?" she asked.

Jake finished two more and then popped to his feet. His gaze flared with raw hunger the moment he saw her standing there in her birthday suit. He grabbed the small towel off the sofa and wiped the sweat from his face. "Please get dressed," he said, but there was definite interest glimmering in his eyes. "I already told you why this wasn't a good idea."

"And I already told you why I don't care." She smiled sweetly. "If you want me dressed…come and dress me."

"Damn it, Kat, this isn't a game. Now get your ass inside that bedroom and put some clothes on," he said, gesturing angrily to the bedroom. "I'm trying to keep you alive. We're not playing games here. How am I supposed to deliver you in one piece if I can't keep my head on straight?"

Kat suddenly felt very foolish and exposed. Here she was, standing naked and available, and he could barely look at her. Maybe she'd misread the signs. Totally possible, she realized with a sinking heart. She was a newbie at this particular social dance and not entirely graceful as it turned out.

She lifted her chin and hoped it didn't wobble as she spun on her heel and returned to the bedroom. This was the epitome of mortification. Offering yourself like you're filet mignon and realizing you're actually those junk pieces of meat the butcher gives to the dogs—yep, mortifying. She slipped her clothes on as quickly as possible and then covered her face with her hands, wondering what she'd been thinking—how could she have been so bold as to think that one night would make a difference in how Jake acted around her. She'd been so sure that things would be different. She'd envisioned waking up to Jake's fevered kisses—particularly that kissing action in the "down there" region—and they'd spend the morning learning each other's bodies like two heathens worshipping an ancient fertility goddess. But no. That's not how it had happened and she should've taken that as a clue to how things would progress. It'd always amazed her that she could be so book-smart and yet when it came to social interactions in the game of life, she was such a damn loser.

Okay, put your game face on, she told herself. Embarrassing situations were not new to her. High school had been one bad experience after another, filled with higher and higher levels of agonizing mortification. She could handle this. Looking at it objectively, she was still the winner. She'd wanted to lose her virginity to someone other than a nerdy bookworm and she'd accomplished that. It hadn't been a wretched experience—the exact opposite actually, so what was she moping about?

Because he didn't want to lounge around like lizards in the sun together? *Pshh. Whatever.* This was just fine.

She'd waited a long time to become a full-fledged woman. And she was going to make the most of it while she still could. Game face on, she marched back into the living room and faced Jake, only this time he was doing crunches and for a long moment, Kat was mesmerized by all those lovely hard ridges of muscle that would've made a model cry with envy. Coming to her senses, she said in a clear voice, "Jake, I've come to reevaluate my position as your temporary lover and, while I was interested in having more sex, I respect your decision to decline my offer of continued coitus—"

"Kat," Jake interrupted, his breathing heavy as he continued to do his crunches. "What are you doing? This isn't necessary. We can just agree to let what happened remain in the past so we can both focus on getting to D.C. alive."

"Oh. Of course." She waited a minute then added, "However, I just want to add my thanks for your thoughtfulness with the mechanics of the act. It was truly very nice."

At that he stopped. "Very nice?"

"Oh, yes. Far better than I expected it to be. Of course, being my first time I really don't know how much better it could be. I guess I'll just have to wait to find out. But now that I think about it, my current situation is going to make dating very difficult. I don't know of many guys who could handle the potential threat of being whacked—is that the right term for it?—just for taking me out to dinner. Maybe you could introduce me to someone like you? Someone with protection experience?"

Jake stopped and his thunderous expression told Kat exactly how he felt about the conversation. "I am not introducing you to anyone. I'm not a dating service. Besides, the last thing you need to be worrying about is dating."

"Says you. I disagree. If you're not willing to educate me, then I will have to find someone who will. Now that I've tasted the forbidden fruit, I can't go back to not knowing what it's like to be touched. I liked it. A lot. And I want more."

Jake climbed to his feet and wiped his face again. "I can't believe we're having this ridiculous conversation," he growled, stalking past her. "I'm done talking about you dating other people and continuing your *sexploration* mission."

"And why is that?" she asked, following him with a frown back into the bedroom where he began stripping. "You shouldn't care. You expressed your desire for me to stop pestering you about you and me."

"Yeah, but that didn't mean I'm throwing the door wide-open for other people to come on in," he countered, plainly irritated, which confused her. "Come on, Kat…this is just… Why don't you put a pin in it for now, okay? We've got bigger problems."

"Fine," she conceded unhappily, and sat on the edge

of the bed. "But I think that's unfair of you to introduce me to the carnal delights only to snatch them away again."

He actually groaned as he disappeared into the bathroom and shut the door, effectively ending his portion of the conversation.

"Well, isn't that rude," she muttered to herself, falling back onto the bed. She supposed Jake was right. There were bigger problems but that didn't change the fact that she wanted to pack every last minute she had with good memories. Most people, when asked what they would do with the last few days, hours, minutes, et cetera, of their life, answered they would spend it with their loved ones. But Kat's loved ones were lost to her. She had no one in this world who cared if she lived or died. Except Jake.

So, if she were asked that same question, she would answer that she'd want to spend it with Jake.

Naked.

Frankly, she didn't understand why Jake couldn't just go along with it. He seemed to enjoy himself. Men didn't fake orgasms, did they? Ugh. Too bad her cell phone didn't have any service because she needed to look up a few things on Google. How could Jake expect her to stuff the genie back into the bottle once it'd tasted freedom? Talk about mission impossible. Kat worried her bottom lip in thought. Well, she'd seduced him once. She could do it again.

Somehow.

* * *

Ridiculous conversation, Jake thought as he scrubbed away the sweat from his workout and from the previous night's activities. How could she blithely talk about sex like that? He didn't consider himself a prude or shy but somehow it made him feel intensely uncomfortable to hear Kat talk about new potential sex partners. As if he would hook her up!

Why not? A voice challenged. Because he wasn't a matchmaker and besides, she had bigger things to worry about than who she was going to date, he countered.

And the very idea of knowing someone else would be satisfying her insatiable hunger really didn't sit well at all with him. *Oh, buddy, you're in trouble.* Yeah, thanks, Captain Obvious. He wanted Kat so bad. It'd taken Herculean strength to climb from that bed and walk away from Kat when all he'd wanted to do was introduce her to even sweeter pleasures. There was an entire world of carnal adventures he could show her and she was an eager student. She didn't shy away from anything like many inexperienced lovers. She ran headlong into a new experience as if she were going to die tomorrow.

Well, genius, she thinks she just might die tomorrow, the voice said dryly, and he wanted to grind out the reason ringing in that damn voice. "I'm not going to let anything happen to her," he said to the steam curling in the shower. He would step in front of a bullet before he let anything happen to her. *Such dedication,* the voice mocked. *And why is that?* "Ah, hell. I'm talking to myself," Jake muttered with disgust. "Bring on the padded cell."

Jake focused his attention on the more pressing details of their situation and forced all thoughts of Kat and her body from his mind. First, he needed to let Nathan know he was here. Second, he needed to find out who either managed to tap into his cell phone coordinates or traced his credit card to find them at that mangy motel. He didn't like the possibilities staring him in the face, and until he had proof, he wouldn't allow himself to jump to conclusions.

He finished scrubbing and exited the shower, satisfied his mind and body were back on track. He needed to stay rigid in his resolve if he wanted them both to come out of this alive, which meant no more giving in to that twisting, aching hunger that seemed to trail his every movement when he so much as glanced at Kat. It was as if a switch had been flipped in his brain and every hormone aimed at making him soft and weak in the head had been released. Nothing a few hundred crunches and push-ups couldn't take care of. Each time he thought of Kat in a way that wasn't appropriate to the situation, he'd just drop and start doing push-ups.

So basically, everytime he looked at her.

Not a very good solution. *Just stop thinking of her that way!* But it was near impossible. She was under his skin in the worst way—like an infection. Wait, no, that wasn't right. Kat was…he didn't even know the right words. She was unlike anyone he'd ever met, so drawing a comparison was useless.

Giving up, Jake exited the bathroom and quickly dressed, surprised to see Kat no longer waiting for him. "Kat?" he called out to her, but hearing no answer he went to the living room. "Kat?" he called again, this time with more urgency but again, no answer. "Damn it, girl, where have you gone?"

He didn't like this. Not one bit. Did he have to tie her to a damn chair to get her to stay put? Hell, maybe he ought to have kept her busy in the bedroom—at least then he'd know where she was!

On that thought, he bolted from the house, grabbing his gun on his way out. If anyone hurt Kat, he'd put a bullet between their eyes.

Chapter 13

"What the hell are you doing out here?" Kat turned at the angry voice at her back and found Jake barreling toward her with a definite scowl that was even deeper than the one he'd been wearing previously. "You shouldn't be out here in the open. Come back inside."

"We're in the middle of nowhere. Who could possibly find us here? It took forever to find it. I doubt anyone would just stumble upon us."

"That goes to show how naive you are. Satellite imagery is everywhere. Haven't you ever heard of Google Earth? Now get inside. That's not a suggestion."

She hated being bossed around but it seemed throughout her life, one person or another was always trying to manipulate her into doing things their way, no matter her objections. First, it was high school bullies, then it was college jerks, then it was overbearing coworkers who seemed to take her aversion to conflict as a green light to push her around. And now it was Jake. However, as much as she wanted to plant her feet and stubbornly refuse to budge, Jake had made a solid point. "It's not easy to be cooped up in a house that's not your own. And I needed a quick breather." She shot him a wounded look—the only indication she would allow that he'd hurt her feelings inside—and then began to trudge back to the house. "What are we supposed to do? Stare at each other? I'm bored. There aren't even any crosswords around. What does your brother do when he comes here? I would go insane."

"I told you, it's his hunting cabin. He comes up here to shoot things."

She grimaced. "I don't approve of sport hunting. I find it unnecessary in this day and age. Humans had to hunt for sustenance but that's not the case any longer. Sport hunting seems cruel."

He shrugged. "I'll let my brother know how you feel. I should warn you—he won't care. Now, please… inside before a sniper manages to get you in his sights and puts a bullet between your eyes."

At that, Kat gasped and hustled back into the house only to flop on the sofa with a groan. "Can't go outside, can't leave, and you aren't interested in passing the time together. I will definitely die of boredom."

"Kat, it's not as if we've been here for weeks," he

pointed out. "Besides, I'm hoping we can pull out of here within a day or two. I have to make contact with my superior and he'll give me direction as to what our next move is. We certainly can't keep hiding from house to house, dodging unknown assailants the entire trip."

"Yeah, that doesn't sound very good to me, either."

"I was about to make that call when I discovered you'd gone. Please do us both a favor and stay put."

She grumbled but agreed. "Fine. Maybe I'll find something to read while you're chatting with your boss."

Jake nodded as if he didn't care what she did as long as she stayed indoors, and then he disappeared into another room, where the phone was presumably, leaving Kat to twiddle her thumbs and slowly descend into madness at this rate. And to think just a few days ago her biggest concern had been catching whoever was stealing her yogurt from the break-room refrigerator. In a place as technologically savvy as Tessara Pharm, how was it that they couldn't get a handle on who was stealing everyone's lunches and snacks? Kat had considered sweet-talking one of the IT guys to rig up a camera system to catch the person in the act but then she remembered that she wasn't very good at sweet-talking or flirting of any kind and resigned herself to the fact that she'd likely never know who was being so damn inconsiderate. However, if she were to wager a guess…it had to be that guy in Research and Development, Archie Kibald. He was always eyeing her Greek yogurt with what appeared like envy. Damn that Archie.

Suddenly tears sprung to her eyes. She missed Archie. She missed her lab. She missed her monkeys. Her life had taken a decided turn for the bizarre and frightening with lightning speed. How was she supposed to navigate such a change? When her parents died, she had her uncle to help smooth out the rough spots, which he did so wonderfully. Now she had no one. She could only depend on herself. And she found that realization too scary for words.

In overly stressful situations, Kat's M.O. was to duck and hide, not turn and face down her attackers. Ugh. Comparatively, she was the exact opposite of Jake. Jake was strong and fearless; she couldn't even imagine a time when he wasn't. What was it like to be fearless? Deep inside, Kat was a quivering ball of goo and she really hated that part about herself. She sighed unhappily and grabbed the first magazine within reaching distance. *Stag and Turkey: The Ultimate Hunter's Companion.*

It wasn't her first choice but it was either that or slip into a boredom-induced coma.

So, Kat prepared to educate herself on the perils of hunting deer and turkey, depending on region.

In the event that their phones were compromised, defense intelligence agents were instructed to memorize a ten-digit global access code, which enabled them to make a call to headquarters no matter where they were in the world. Jake had always found the code tedious—

because the number changed quarterly as to avoid fraud or theft—but he was grateful for it now. He quickly dialed the ten-digit access code and was immediately routed to headquarters and then to his superior's office.

"Jake Isaacs," he said as soon as Miles picked up the phone.

"Jake, thank God. You fell off the radar and we were afraid you'd been compromised. Is our scientist still with you?"

"Affirmative," Jake answered, but Miles's possessive tone rubbed Jake the wrong way. The fact that Jake even noticed the subtle inflection gave him pause. This was the cost of blurring the lines between him and a target, and he wanted to swear with irritation at his lack of control. "Yes, Kat is with me and she is unharmed."

"Kat? Becoming a little informal with a target? Do you feel that's wise?"

"She prefers that I call her Kat, and it puts her at ease in a stressful situation. I figured it was best."

"Ah. Excellent thinking. Best to keep her amiable."

Jake didn't respond because he was becoming more and more uncomfortable with the slant of the conversation. He didn't know Miles Jogan very well, but he knew he was a highly decorated officer before he'd come to the defense intelligence team and he'd been personally hand-selected by the highest ranking officer in their division. He had no reason to question him, which made Jake think that he was putting too many personal feelings into the mission because of what he and Kat had done. Shame colored his cheeks and he was glad Miles couldn't read his expression over the phone. "Since the incident at the motel, we've been forced to hole up out of sight for safety reasons. We're going to need an extraction seeing as Kat is afraid to fly and she's allergic to sedatives."

"Well, as much as I'd like to accommodate Dr. Odgers's desire to drive to D.C., what's more important than her comfort is her safety."

"I understand but I know Kat isn't going to board a plane willingly."

"I hear you, but you're not hearing me. Her compliance is not dependent on her willingness. I'm sure we have a drug that will take into consideration her allergies and that will help ease her anxiety. I was willing to allow this plan to drive as long as her safety was not at risk. She is simply too valuable to take chances at this point. Can you get to the Reno airport?"

Jake's gut tightened with discomfort. "Yes."

"Good. I will have transport awaiting Dr. Odgers. Your job is to bring her there. After that, she'll be transferred into the custody of Agent Camille Stephens. From there, you will be reassigned."

"I respectfully request to remain with Dr. Odgers until she arrives in D.C.," Jake said. "I feel she will be more willing to comply with me around."

"Not necessary. After she's given the sedative, she won't even realize who's around her. I expect to see you on the tarmac at 6 a.m. tomorrow. Can you handle that?"

"Yes, sir."

"Good man. See you tomorrow."

Jake hung up and stared at the floor, perplexed. Reassigned? Why? His job was to bring Kat to D.C., but now she was being transferred to Camille Stephens? He knew Camille, she was the same rank as him, with an impeccable service record. He knew her to be an excellent markswoman and she could break a kneecap without breaking a sweat. In short, she was smart, capable and deadly—which should be enough to keep Kat safe but it wasn't good enough for him.

Too bad. Nobody was asking his opinion and Miles had already pushed him on to the next assignment for reasons Jake couldn't fathom. Something felt off, his intuition warned, but the logical side of his thought process berated him for even daring to question a superior officer. For whatever reasons Miles had reassigned him, they were probably good ones.

Bullshit, that stubborn voice said. *Listen to your gut.*

No. Jake put his trust in his superior and that's where it would stay. He'd just have to get right with the decision.

If that was the case, he needed to tell Kat. He could already picture her face blanching at the news and the fear widening her pupils. She'd probably bolt. He'd have to find a way to get her to the Reno airport without alarming her. She'd have to trust him completely. His stomach churned as he realized what he'd have to do. Kat wanted him—and he wanted Kat. The solution to his dilemma was underhanded and borderline unethical but he had a reputation for getting the job done and he wasn't about to fail.

If bending Kat to his will meant succumbing to his baser desires…he'd do it.

The trick would be to keep his emotions out of it, because even though he put on a good show, Kat was getting under his skin in the worst way—and he was starting to like it.

Chapter 14

Kat was flipping through another one of those horrid hunting magazines when Jake returned from making his telephone call. It was hard enough to keep her mind focused on a normal day but on a day when she was so bored she wanted to scream—impossible. She tried not to stare with longing at Jake's near-perfect form but the man was something of a god. How was it that he was still single? Logically, she knew that if a man with Jake's good looks and superior physique was still single there was probably something terribly wrong with him. For the life of her, she couldn't even imagine what those flaws might be.

"Why are you single?" she asked, going straight for the jugular. If she had to spend time in an enclosed space with a person she was wildly attracted to but couldn't touch, she could at least make the time interesting. "You have to know that it is a bit odd that a person such as yourself would remain single. Men like you are a rarity, from what I can tell."

"What do you mean?"

"Exactly what I said. You're good-looking, you have a good job, you're smart… What's wrong with you? There has to be something that keeps women away otherwise you would've been snapped up with a ring on your finger faster than you can blink. All the good guys are always taken—it's a cliché for a reason."

He smirked. "So I'm defective because I'm single?" At that she shrugged, because sometimes the truth was unattractive but valid just the same. Jake sighed as if amused that he was explaining his lack of attachments. "If you recall, I wasn't always single. Remember I told you I had a long-term girlfriend and things didn't work out?"

"Yes, I do remember that but I don't buy it. I can't imagine anyone walking away from you. So that means you walked away from her. I could believe that. Maybe that's your issue. Commitment."

"What makes you think I have an issue? Maybe it just didn't work out because we weren't right together. Sometimes that happens. Haven't you ever had a relationship that didn't gel for whatever reason? Doesn't mean there is anything wrong with either one of you. It just means you weren't right for one another."

"My dating knowledge up to this point has been empirical. I haven't had much opportunity to date, hence the reason I was still a virgin. It wasn't that I was protecting my *feminine treasure,* it was that I didn't have anyone in my life who was interested in going to that next level of intimacy. And if I'm being honest, I wasn't all that interested in dating, because I was so focused on finding a cure and perfecting MCX-209. Now that I realize it was such a failure I wish had spent more time dating."

"Dating isn't all it's cracked up to be. Believe it or not, I've been on a few dates since my breakup. I tried to get out there, mix it up. But I don't have the patience for the dating scene. I find idle conversation unnecessary, time-consuming and boring. Kind of makes it hard to meet people when you find the first-date ritual tedious."

"Since you hate dating so much, how did you meet your long-term girlfriend?"

"We were in the army together. We were sort of thrown together and it was convenient."

Katherine frowned. "That's not very romantic."

Jake laughed. "Yeah, that's what she said. I guess I'm just not a romantic guy. I'm more of a straightforward kind of person. If I like you, I tell you. I don't beat around the bush. And I don't like games. So, there you have it. Me in a nutshell—not romantic, not the flowers-and-chocolate kind of guy. Maybe that's what's wrong with me."

"What do you have against flowers?"

"I feel they're a useless waste of money. They're expensive and they die a few days later. I don't see the point."

Kat stilled for a long moment. She loved flowers and no one had ever sent her flowers, but she used to watch with a fair amount of secret envy as other female coworkers had received pretty things by courier sometimes, and it'd made her wish she had someone in her life to send her a flower or two. "The point of flowers is that they're pretty and they smell nice and they make a woman feel as if she's wanted and appreciated."

"There are other ways to show a woman she's wanted and appreciated, aside from giving her something that's going to die in a few days," Jake said softly. She looked up to find him staring at her in a way that made her breath catch. "Do you really love flowers that much?" She nodded and he sighed. "Do you have a preference or will any flower do?"

"I love all flowers—no preference. I want to know what it's like to feel cherished, as if you're the only woman in the world who exists for that one person. I want to feel noticed."

"And flowers do this for you?"

She fiddled with the magazine, then admitted, "I wouldn't actually know. I've never received flowers for any reason but I like the idea of it, so until I know otherwise, I would like flowers delivered to me."

"That's good to know," Jake murmured, leaning in to close the gap between them. She dropped the magazine from her fingers when she realized with a rapidly beating heart that Jake was going to kiss her. She wanted this more than anything but her confusion threatened to ruin all the fluttery good feelings in her stomach. Jake noted her reservation and pulled back with a subtle frown. "What's wrong?" he asked.

"What are you doing? This morning I threw myself at you and you pushed me away, which I might add, was a terrible blow to my really fragile ego, and now you're coming at me like you want to kiss me and you have that look in your eyes like I'm something special and I'm just confused. Don't get me wrong, I like that look on you but you're running hot and cold and I don't know how to handle that. I'm no good at these kinds of games, so if you're playing me you have an unfair advantage. And I need to know what's going on before we go any further."

"What's going on is that I feel something for you that I shouldn't and I'm consumed with the need to touch and feel your lips and your skin. But I'll stop if you don't want me to go any further. I'm not playing any games. What you see is what you get with me. The fact of the matter is I want you, Kat, and it may be wrong but I don't want to stop."

Kat wanted to sing with joy. Basically Jake had just said everything she would've wanted him to say but something still felt off. "I don't mean to be a stickler but what changed?"

"Does it matter?" Jake leaned in and placed a soft,

sweet kiss along her jawline. "What matters is you and me. This moment. Right now."

Yeah, that was easy to believe, but she couldn't handle the thought that Jake was playing games with her. If it were true, it would cripple her and she wasn't willing to take that chance, not even for Jake.

"I don't believe you," she admitted, hating that she just couldn't go along with whatever the moment was. It was the scientist in her. Two plus two always equaled four and the logic was hard to ignore. This morning Jake had pushed her away under no uncertain terms and now he was practically trying to seduce her—which frankly wouldn't be hard but something didn't ring true. "Tell me the truth. What is going on? Just tell me. I can handle it."

Jake sighed and pulled away. "Kat, you're overthinking things just like I was overthinking things this morning. I live my life to a certain code and it's bad business to cross professional lines with a target. I can't be objective with you when we're busy tearing each other's clothes off. Doesn't work that way. I don't know why I feel the way I do with you. Trust me, I wish I didn't. It's really messing up my ability to think straight but I can't deny that you bring out something in me that I've never felt and it's like a drug. And maybe like a drug it's really bad for me, I don't know. All I do know is that I've been consumed with this need to be around you. Does that answer your question? Do you still think I'm trying to play games? Because I'm not. I'm not that guy. I don't know what I feel for you but I know it's real and it's seriously powerful. I don't know how much time we have together. All I know is that I want to spend this time with you right now."

And just like that the magic of Jake's words penetrated the wall of resistance and every barrier she felt around her dissolved. Kat sank into his arms and allowed him to drag her into his lap, and this time his kisses were not sweet or soft but hard and demanding and they sent ripples of need spiraling through her like crazy fireworks shooting up into the sky to burst into brilliant arrays of color and sound. *Please don't let this be a lie,* she thought to herself as she succumbed to the wave of desire Jake created with his touch. *Please let this be real. I couldn't bear if this was all a lie.*

He was a bastard. Plain and simple. There were no two ways about it. And he might even be going to hell, but in the end he was there to do a job and he never failed when it came to a mission. Still, he was walking the line between keeping himself separate from the desperate feelings of need and want that sprang to life the minute Kat softened in his arms and the cold hard logical part of his brain that encouraged him to do whatever necessary to gain her trust. This was more than physical and he knew it. That was the part that scared him. He craved her sweet gasps as he plundered her flesh and wanted to swallow every cry into his soul. The thundering of his heart in his ears as he clutched her to him was no act and it was fruitless to try and pretend otherwise.

"This sex stuff is addictive," Kat said, breathing hard as she stared up at the ceiling with dreamy eyes. "If I'd known that it could be this great, I might've ditched the science stuff and gone into the sordid life of a call girl."

He laughed, knowing she was joking but he did swell with a little male pride that he'd introduced her to sex with such success. "I'll take that as a compliment," he said, and she rolled into his arms, propping herself on his chest. He grinned at how adorable she looked mussed and thoroughly tousled after their lovemaking. "I pride myself in ensuring a job is done right."

"Oh, yes, you certainly did that. You rocked it. You could medal in monkey business. But then you must know you're pretty good."

"Well, I like to think that I have a certain talent for some things," he answered with a half-cocky smile. How could he not feel like crowing when his woman was singing his praises? He laughed and tugged her on top of him. She pushed off his chest and sat atop him, grinning, her small breasts perfect handfuls with their upturned nipples and soft, rounded cups. Her hair drifted around her shoulders in fine, baby-soft wisps and her green eyes danced with wonder and merriment. He took a mental snapshot so he could always remember her this way and tucked it away in a private lockbox.

He placed his hands on her small hips and rocked her gently against his groin, enjoying the way her cheeks flushed and her mouth opened slightly on a groan. "How could a woman like you escape the marriage trap?" he asked, half wondering whether the men in her circles were plainly blind if they couldn't see Kat's beauty and charm. "You're breathtaking."

Kat opened her half-mast eyes and the building pleasure seeped from her expression as if she were recalling a painful moment and he immediately regretted making the comment. Kat placed her hands on his and pushed them away from her hips so she could climb off him. He sat up and stared after her with concern. "What's wrong?" he asked.

"All my life I've been told how plain I am and I grew to accept it. Any time a guy made mention of my looks, it was only to mock them. My mouse-brown hair isn't luxurious or thick, it doesn't hold a curl and surely doesn't snag a man's attention when it's up or down, and my eyes are a strange green that one guy actually told me were creepy. So when you tell me something like I'm breathtaking, I don't know how to react to that because I don't feel comfortable accepting a compliment for what it is. I don't know how to trust a compliment from a man."

"Whoever told you your eyes were creepy is an idiot. Your eyes are the most striking feature about you— aside from those near-perfect breasts, of course." Kat blushed a beautiful shade of pink and he smiled. "You think I'm kidding, but I'm not. Your breasts are… *magnificent*. A perfect mouthful—"

"Okay, I get the point," Kat interrupted around an embarrassed smile that he found incredibly alluring. "You like boobs. Sorry to break it to you but most guys do."

"No," he corrected her. "I like *your* boobs. Big difference between just any woman's boobs and yours."

"Oh." She flashed another embarrassed smile as she ducked her head. "You were saying?"

"Basically, it comes down to this. You may have been a homely child or a plain teenager but you sure as hell are anything but as a full-grown woman and that's a fact. Anyone who tells you differently is either blind or just plain stupid and not worth your time, anyway."

"Why are you telling me this?" Kat asked, her eyes wide and her expression vulnerable.

"Because you need to hear it," he answered gruffly, hating that people in her past had damaged her self-worth. Jake knew how it felt to be stomped on in the self-worth department and if it were within his power, he'd erase the pain Kat had suffered as a result. But that was out of his control. All he could do was say what needed to be said in this moment because that's all he had.

He could feel the doubt radiating from her expressive eyes and he wished he could reassure her that he would never lie to her, so that she could accept his words as truth, but he couldn't bring himself to make that assurance. Instead, he gently pulled her to him and placed a kiss on her mouth that conveyed how he felt with the power of his lips and tongue and hoped that she could hear the message without words.

The fact was he didn't trust himself.

And if she knew what he planned to do, she wouldn't trust him, either.

Chapter 15

"Is everything okay?" his brother, Nathan, asked over the phone line. "What's going on?"

"I don't really know. Still trying to figure that out. There was the possibility that my cell phone had been compromised so I had to ditch it after our first location had been discovered. I needed a place to hole up until I received new orders. I wanted to give you a quick call to let you know I was using the cabin. I didn't want you to think someone had broken into your place. Oh, and as an aside, I hate your compost toilet."

"Yeah, emptying the liquid compartment is a bitch but it does the job and that's all that matters."

"I guess. Thanks for letting me stay here. I owe you one."

"No problem. Are you gonna tell me the mission? What's going on?"

"It's classified."

"Don't give me that bullshit. You know I have clearance."

"Different departments, different clearance."

"Cut the crap, Jake. There's a fine line between what my department did and what yours does."

Jake bristled, taking immediate offense. Nathan's branch, the U.S. Department of Informational Development, or ID for short, was run by a bunch of egomaniacs with personal agendas who were allowed to run amok for too long in covert, shady operations. The Department of Intelligence wasn't anything like that, aside from the fact that the U.S. government paid both their bills. Add in the fact that ID was recently shut down as a result of the aforementioned offenses…yeah, Jake took particular offense that Nathan would even suggest that they were similar in nature, but whatever, he wasn't calling to debate that subject. "You and Jaci good?" he asked, changing the subject.

"We're fine. Thanks for asking but I know what you're doing," Nathan said, calling Jake on his deflection. "I know it's been a long time since we were close but I can still tell when you're not being honest. Do you need help?"

"Too bad I couldn't tell when you were lying to my face," Jake muttered, immediately wishing he could take it back. He still had some unresolved issues with his big brother and it was hard not to take offense to even the smallest thing between them. "I've got it under control. If I need you, I'll call you."

"No, you won't. Stubborn little shit." Nathan sighed. "I know we haven't had that sit-down chat that we should have but don't let your pride get in the way of asking for help. I've got resources that you can use. All you have to do is ask."

"What resources could you have that I don't?" Jake asked, irritated. "Besides, all I have to do is deliver Kat and my part of this mission is over. I've been reassigned to something else."

"Who is this Kat?"

"Her name is Dr. Katherine Odgers and she works for Tessara Pharmaceuticals."

"Well, that's a name that rings a bell and one that brings trouble with it. What's going on with Tessara Pharm now?"

"You're going to keep asking until you get something out of me, aren't you?" Jake asked. "I told you it was classified."

"Fine. You know I can find out if I want to. I've got connections, too. I just want to make sure you're all right, Jakey."

The scar Jake thought had long since ceased to hurt suddenly burned like fire. "I told you not to call me that. Listen, I have to go. Thanks again for the use of the cabin. I'll put a couple of bucks in the mail for your trouble."

Nathan exhaled as if Jake were being difficult. "Don't worry about it. I just wish you would trust me enough to tell me what's going on. I have a feeling— a bad feeling—that something is about to go down."

Jake smirked. "Don't quit your day job. Last time I checked you weren't psychic, so stop wringing your hands and relax. This job is almost over and I'll be glad when it's done."

"Do me a favor and call me when you're done. I want to make sure that this goes down by the numbers."

"You don't have to play the part of the big brother any longer. I can take care of myself. This was simply a courtesy call, not a plea for help."

"Jake, I screwed up in the big brother department. I should've been there for you but I wasn't. If you'll let me, I'll do my best to be there for you from now on. I thought maybe things might've changed between us after I almost died during that last operation but I'm getting the message loud and clear that nothing's changed."

Jake ground the sting from his eyes. What the hell was wrong with him? One phone call from his brother and he was ready to bawl like a baby. "Yeah, whatever. I'll call you later." But as Jake hung up he wondered why he didn't just tell Nathan that he probably wouldn't call and he had a hard time with this whole "let's let bygones be bygones" crap because he couldn't quite forgive his brother for leaving him behind. Maybe that made him a jerk, maybe he was being petty, but Nathan could've spared Jake the misery of being left behind with their father. How was he supposed to forgive Nathan for willfully walking away, knowing what was going to happen to him when he left? Jake didn't know the answer and maybe that's why he resisted all overtures from Nathan to try to make amends.

Shake it off, Jake told himself. He had bigger problems.

"Who were you talking to?" Kat asked as she dried her hair. "Was that your brother?"

He nodded. "I just wanted to give him a heads-up that we were here and not burglars."

"That was nice of you. What's your brother like?"

"I wouldn't know. We're not close."

"Well, you're close enough to crash at his cabin at a moment's notice," Kat pointed out. "I think I'd like to meet him. I bet he's a very interesting individual."

Fat chance of that. Jake couldn't see Kat having reason to meet Nathan at all but to admit that would bring up questions he couldn't answer. "Maybe sometime," he lied, quickly changing the subject. "I have good news. I managed to make contact with my superior and he's arranged an extraction. All we have to do is meet him at a designated point and transport will be waiting."

"What kind of transport?"

"A government vehicle."

"Not a plane?"

He smiled and lied through his teeth. "No, it's a car."

Kat's relieved smile sliced through his gut. "Oh, thank goodness. Great! That means no more eating

MREs, right? I don't think I can choke down another at this point. What time do we leave?"

"We have to meet them at 6 a.m. tomorrow."

"That will give us just enough time to get to know each other a little better."

"Girl, I don't know how much better we can get to know each other. We know each other pretty intimately by this point."

"I'm not sure about that. You've told me a little bit about your childhood but not much. If you share some more details, I'll share some of mine, too. In college I had to take a psychology class to satisfy my major, which I found completely ridiculous seeing as I was going into a totally separate field but anyway, I actually learned a few interesting things about people in that class that I would only admit to you right now."

"And why is that?" he asked, curious in spite of his intuition warning him to shut down her request.

"Because I was quite vocal in my opinion that the class was useless and I loathe the idea of looking like a hypocrite."

A smile tugged at his lips but he quelled it when he realized she was completely serious about digging deeper into his psyche. "Let's not. Some stories just aren't very interesting."

"I don't believe that for a second. Men like you don't spring up from the dirt. They are shaped and molded by their experiences. I know your childhood wasn't happy, that much I figured out. What happened? What went so wrong?"

"It's really not something I like to talk about." He gave her a hard look. "Please drop it." It wasn't a suggestion and Kat knew it. She appeared disappointed by his reaction but he couldn't open that box. He worked hard to distance himself from that weak, scared boy, and talking about what it'd been like during those wretched years only served to remind him how pathetic he'd been.

And the thought of revealing that side of him to Kat scared him to death.

Jake was on edge. He smiled at her jokes and made small talk but by the time 5:00 a.m. rolled around the following morning, he was no longer putting on the act that everything was okay.

"What aren't you telling me?" Kat asked, almost afraid to know as they prepared to go.

He looked at her sharply. "What are you talking about?"

"I mean, there's something about you that's different. You're preoccupied with something."

"Of course I'm preoccupied. We're about to leave a safe zone to venture out in the open again. My primary concern is keeping you safe. I know you're safe here, but out there? I don't know who's after us or who compromised the security of my network. That makes me a bit jumpy."

She bit her lip. "I understand. For a second I was worried I'd done something wrong."

Jake paused and pulled her to him. "Listen to me. You've done nothing wrong. Nothing up to this point has been your fault. You're caught in a bad situation. That's all. Okay?" She nodded and he swept a quick kiss across her lips. "Now let's get moving. We have about an hour drive before we reach the extraction point."

Kat nodded again and finished stuffing what little belongings she had into her pack. "You're going to be with me, right?" she asked.

"Of course," he answered, but skewed his gaze away from her in a way that immediately set her nerves on alert. He caught her wary look and tried to assure her. "Your safety is a top priority for everyone in my agency. We're on your side. Just remember that, okay?"

"Okay," she said, but she couldn't shake the feeling that Jake wasn't being entirely honest with her. Her intuition was screaming at her to press him harder for information but after the sweet way he touched her, her heart desperately wanted to take his words at face value. "So where is the extraction point?" she asked.

"About an hour from here so we better get moving."

It didn't escape her notice that Jake evaded her question and answered vaguely. She didn't know what to think about his strange behavior. She wanted to believe him, which meant she had to put aside her misgivings and trust that he had her best interests at heart.

Jake locked the house up and they climbed into the

old Camaro. As they put miles between themselves and the hunting cabin, Kat couldn't shake the feeling that she'd better treasure what had happened within those four walls because things were about to change— dramatically.

Chapter 16

"Why are we taking the Reno International Airport exit?" Kat asked, a note of strain in her voice. "What's going on?" Her fingers had curved into claws as she dug into the seat. "Jake? You said we were going by car."

"Yes, but no one is going to notice a car amid hundreds. An airport is good cover."

"Oh," Kat said, visibly relaxing. "For a second I was worried."

Jake nodded, ignoring that ever-present wrench in his gut each time he lied to Kat. He told himself his subterfuge was a necessary evil in order to keep her safe. With an unknown assailant on their tail, there was no way they could safely make the trek by car to D.C.

"I didn't used to be scared of flying until my parents

died," Kat explained while she watched the planes soar overhead as they took off and landed. Jake navigated the terminal, going to a private plane area where he knew his replacement would be waiting. "But you see, my parents didn't actually die skydiving. They never got the opportunity to jump from the plane. An engine blew on the tiny plane they were using and they plummeted to the ground. It was determined to be a freak accident. I know they say that flying is safer than driving but having lost my parents to a plane crash, I don't believe it. My fear is probably a bit irrational but..." She stopped when the car pulled into a hangar and she saw a sleek black vehicle and a sharp private plane waiting. She turned to Jake, her eyes wide. "Jake?"

"Come on," he instructed, and climbed from the car. She had no choice but to follow. He walked briskly to an impeccably dressed woman with exotic features who made Kat feel like a nondescript twig on a tree with a million branches. Kat wanted to cling to Jake but knew to do that would be to reveal their intimacy level— something Jake would disapprove of—and so she stood rigidly straight by herself as Jake and the woman talked. Maybe this wasn't what it seemed. Maybe the woman came by plane and the car was awaiting them. It was possible. Jake gestured for Kat to come closer. "Dr. Katherine Odgers, this is agent Camille Stephens. She will be your contact from this point forward."

"What?" Kat looked wildly to Jake for an explanation but he wasn't looking at her any longer. In fact, he seemed as if he were loath to look at her at all. Tears stung her eyes. "You promised me you were going with me."

"Plans change. It was out of my control."

"I don't believe you. I think you knew all along, which is why you've been acting so weird."

He didn't get the chance to refute her accusation. The woman, Camille Stephens, stepped forward and introduced herself with a cold, efficient smile. "I'm Agent Stephens. I will be seeing to your safety for the second half of this mission."

She wanted to refuse but seeing as Jake had just washed his hands free of her without a single ounce of regret, she didn't know how she could. Plus, she was spitting mad at Jake for blatantly lying to her face. If he lied about one thing, chances were, he'd lied about other things, as well.

Two large men flanked Camille Stephens and made Kat uncomfortable, but she figured they were bodyguards whose purpose was to make people think twice about making trouble so she tried to relax.

"We're here to make sure you arrive safely in Washington, D.C., and the best way to facilitate that is to fly," Camille said calmly as if she hadn't just blown the last bit of Kat's ability to remain sane in this messed-up situation. Kat began to shake her head in protest but Camille kept talking as if Kat's terror weren't an issue. Camille gestured to her bodyguards and they began advancing on Kat. "We've been made aware of your phobia and we have prepared something to ease your anxiety. If you'll allow us to administer the sedative, we'll be on our way."

"Hell, no," Kat said, backing away and shooting a look to Jake for help, but he wasn't going to lift a finger to help and tears stung her eyes. This was a nightmare. "Don't you dare touch me with that syringe. I have rights. I'm an American citizen!"

The bodyguards had Kat in their grip faster than she could run away and soon they were dragging Kat, kicking and struggling, toward Camille who was holding a syringe as if it were a completely normal occurrence to drug someone unconscious. Within seconds, Camille had plunged the needle in Kat's arm and it was done. "Jake! Oh, my God! Why aren't you helping me? I can't believe you would let them do this to me." Her words were already slurring but her ears worked just fine. Jake didn't say a word. At least not to her.

"Do you have a medic on board in case your little knockout drug causes her to have a bad reaction?"

"Of course. She'll be fine." Camille handed Jake a manila packet. "Your new assignment. This one you should be able to handle. Be aware that there is a timely element to this one. Tardiness is ill-advised."

Jake glared at Camille and tucked the packet under his arm. "Take care of her."

"Of course I will. She's a national treasure. But you seem overly attached. Maybe I should let Miles know you got too involved with the target of this mission?"

"Mind your own business. Just take care of her. If a hair on her head is harmed, I'm putting the blame on you."

Camille chuckled at that as if his warning were of little consequence and if Kat's tongue had been working, she would've yelled that it served him right but she could no more say her piece than say her own name. And she was fading fast. Her last thought before she dropped off a cliff into total blackness was a pitiful cry for Jake's betrayal.

Jake immediately put miles between him and the airport, not wanting to remember the expression on Kat's face when she realized he'd betrayed her. *It's for her own good,* he told himself. Her safety—not personal feelings—was paramount, but as he drove in the opposite direction something kept tugging at his mind. Something that didn't feel right and had nothing to do with his personal feelings. This was a warning in the back of his mind alerting him to a potentially dangerous situation.

It was something Camille had said. She'd called Kat a "national treasure." What did that mean? To his knowledge the mission was to secure Kat for her own safety. The plan had been to relocate her with a different identity so she could live out her life like a normal person and not have to always look over her shoulder for whomever might want to appropriate her for their own purposes.

So if the plan remained that Kat was going to be relocated with a new identity, why would she be called a national treasure? Breaking it down even further Jake picked apart the words *national* and *treasure*. For Kat to have value to the U.S. government, that would mean they were planning to use her knowledge for something else—which also meant she was not going to be relocated or given a new identity. A queasy, greasy knot congealed in his stomach as he wondered if he'd just handed over Kat to the wrong people. But that couldn't be, because Miles Jogan, his boss, had sent Camille to collect Kat and there was no way that someone as highly decorated as Miles was crooked. *You're being ridiculous. There is no conspiracy theory. Stop reading more into the situation than is warranted.*

Kat was protected, that's what mattered. Sure it wasn't an ideal situation but at least he didn't have to worry about a sniper putting her in his sights. He was a government agent, first and foremost. He was the job—and the job was him. If he hadn't given in to his primal instincts, he wouldn't be faced with the situation and he wouldn't be questioning the orders. It was not his job to question. It was his job to deliver.

Perhaps Camille was right and he should let Miles know he'd compromised the mission in some way. *Well, now you're just talking crazy,* the voice chastised. There was no sense in tanking his entire career over one decision when in the end everything worked out as it should. But had it? He didn't know that everything had worked out. All he knew was that he had handed over Kat, someone he'd come to care about, to that coldhearted bitch Camille Stephens in the hopes that everything was on the up-and-up.

Stop it. Focus. There was a new assignment to complete—that's where his attention needed to be. Reaching over to the passenger seat he picked up the manila packet and ripped it open, steadying the wheel with his knee as he pulled the paperwork and scanned the contents.

He frowned. This type of assignment was beneath his rank. This was rookie stuff. Delivering paperwork? Now he was a clerk? What the hell did he do to piss Miles off so badly? Had he inadvertently offended his superior? Or was it that Miles blamed him for the situation getting bungled with Kat? Jake grumbled, his mood souring even further. This was all manner of messed-up crap. But he'd do the job because he always did what he was tasked to do.

At least he was headed in the right direction. The exchange spot was only a few miles from the airport, according to the directions in the packet. Without his phone he couldn't double-check the GPS. No problem. Before GPS, he was a pretty good navigator. He didn't have any worries that he wouldn't find the location.

Just as he expected, he found the location—a small deserted gas station on the outskirts of a lonely highway—and waited. Right on time, a sleek black government car rolled up. Jake exited his vehicle at the same time as the other agent. "The sky is blue," the agent said by way of greeting.

Jake answered, "And the mud is red."

The agent nodded and Jake began to walk forward with the paperwork but that same sense that kept telling him something was wrong when Camille came to collect Kat began shrieking in his head and it was that minute, split-second warning that caught the quick movement by the agent as he pulled his gun.

Jake dove just in time to avoid getting shot in the gut and pulled his own gun, burying a bullet in the agent's head. It'd all happened so fast that for a moment Jake wasn't sure if his bullet had hit the mark or if the agent's bullet had hit his. But when he saw the agent fall and not get back up, and after a quick body check, Jake realized he was unharmed. He quickly scrambled to his feet, breathing heavy and pissed as hell. He'd been set up. This was no drop-off and pickup. This was a designated hit. Someone had wanted him out of the way. And he had a feeling it had everything to do with Kat.

After a quick search of the agent's body, he pulled the man's cell phone and wallet. He did a quick scan of the cell for any messages that might pertain to who had given him the order and, finding it empty, he crushed it beneath his booted heel, knowing that the GPS would send them here. Then he took whatever cash the agent had and tossed the wallet. While the agent's car was a sleek ride with all of the niceties, Jake also knew it was equipped with GPS and whoever wanted him dead would be able to find him quite nicely if he took off in that car.

He doubled back to the old Camaro and jumped inside, hitting the gas hard. He had to find Kat before it was too late. And he had to find out if Miles was the security breach or if he was unaware that there was a rat in the organization. But how? How was he going to find out the answers he needed without getting himself killed for asking? He thought of his brother, Nathan, and realized he may have pushed away his brother's offer of help prematurely. He was too desperate to be embarrassed, thank God. All that mattered was fixing the colossal mistake he'd made in handing over Kat when his gut had warned him against it.

He should've listened to his instincts.

He could only hope he hadn't just sold Kat into a lifetime of slavery under the guise of protection.

Chapter 17

Kat opened her eyes to stare blearily at her surroundings. It took a moment to remember what had happened but everything came back quickly once she focused her mind. She rubbed her mouth and wiped away the dried drool, thankful that she was alone.

Of course, Jake was nowhere to be found. She squeezed her eyes shut as a wave of pain followed. She still couldn't believe he'd so quickly betrayed her. Had everything been a lie? Had he set out to seduce her so that she would be easy to manipulate? Of course he had. She'd known something was different. He'd gone from pushing her away to practically dragging her into his arms. And she'd been happy to soak up every lie that he'd sent her way, because she wanted to believe.

A ragged sob caught in her chest. She wanted to believe someone like Jake had felt the same way about her as she felt about him. How could she be so stupid, so naive? She should've known that it was all an act. Lord knew she had plenty of experiences in her life that would've supported her theory.

She surveyed the small room. At least she was no longer on a plane. Whatever they had given her had done the trick. Damn government, they had access to all sorts of drugs. Only God knew if it was safe or not. Chances were because it wasn't released to the general public, it had some quirky side effects. Hopefully she didn't start growing a sixth finger or something strange like that because of it. Or, as in the case with MCX-209, she lost all her memories.

The door opened and Camille walked in. The woman was almost too beautiful to look at, and Kat was momentarily curious if she was the kind of woman who Jake preferred. Who cared? She didn't want to care but she did. She might've fallen in love with Jake. Maybe it was just infatuation. But right now her heart felt as if it were caving in and it was all Jake's fault.

"Here are some new clothes," Camille said, tossing the bundle to Kat. "There is a shower, please use it. You have a meeting with Miles Jogan in one hour."

"Who is Miles Jogan?" Kat asked. "Where is Jake?"

A thin smile spread across Camille's lips. "Jake is no longer your concern. Miles Jogan is the man you're going to want to impress."

"And why is that?"

Again that thin smile that Kat didn't trust one bit. "One hour." And then Camille left. There was the distinct sound of a lock sliding into place and Kat knew she was no guest.

"I'm not feeling very safe," she muttered to herself as she shook out the bundle, which turned out to be nothing short of prison garb in lab coat–white. The clothes were functional, nothing fancy, without pockets. *Definitely not a guest here.* But at least the clothes were clean. She scooped them up and found her way to the small bathroom and after a shower and clean clothes she felt at the very least refreshed, if not still completely confused. Right on schedule, Camille reappeared an hour later to collect her. Camille gave Kat a once-over and without saying a word, directed her to follow.

"Are you going to tell me what's going on? I think I figured out that what Jake thought was going to happen is not actually going to happen, so if you wouldn't mind cluing me in that would be great."

"Miles will answer your questions." Camille opened the door and pushed Kat through it. Kat scowled at Camille but the impressive-looking man sitting behind a large expensive desk in the room snagged her attention. Handsome, older—he reminded her of George Clooney with a couple more years on him—and for some reason she didn't trust him at all. "Ahh, Dr. Odgers, so pleasant to finally make your acquaintance. I'm a huge fan of your work and that clever mind of yours."

"And what work would that be?" she asked, not charmed one bit.

"Why that would be the work that's going to change the world, of course."

"My work was a fiasco. MCX-209 was meant to improve the lives of Alzheimer's patients. The drug was a dismal failure."

"Yes, unfortunate that. However the applications for MCX-209 are imminently bigger than the application for its intended use. I'm sure you know that in the hands of the military, this drug could change the course of human history. Imagine all the good we could do with a drug like this. Take a minute to consider if we'd had a drug like this to use against Adolf Hitler. Imagine wiping out racism, genocide, dictators…we could completely eradicate all of the ugliness in the world with one simple drug. No side effects, no death, just desired results."

"Are you nuts? What about free will, Constitutional rights? You can't wipe away someone's memories just because they don't follow the same rules as the rest of us. It's a slippery slope and one I'm not willing to travel with my research."

Kat couldn't believe she was having this ethical debate with a high-ranking government official. "How does someone like you get so corrupt?" she asked, curious. "Is it the power? The money? Did you start out bad or was it a gradual moral and ethical disintegration?"

Miles smiled as if her question amused him but his

gaze frosted over. "Careful. The questions we ask…we might not like the answers."

"Well, I already don't like you, so I doubt anything you say could influence my opinion."

"For such a tiny, plain thing, you sure have a lot of fire."

Kat winced at the judgment in Miles's stare but she lifted her chin, refusing to be cowed by old fears and insecurities. Even though she wanted to kick Jake in the shins—really hard—for what he did to her, it was his voice telling her that she was beautiful that gave her strength. "Let me take a guess…greed? Kinda cliché, though, don't you think? Government salary not enough for you? Are you the faux Hollywood-type? Wanting to pretend you're someone with lots of money so you can spend your dotage with bubble-headed bimbos young enough to be your granddaughters? So gross. I'd warn you that there's no dignity in that but I think you sold out your dignity a long time ago."

"You have no sense of self-preservation," Miles observed, then smiled. "It's a good thing we're looking out for you. Otherwise, you might find yourself in a dangerous situation."

"Oh, baloney. You don't care about my safety and if I put my health and welfare in your hands, I'd be dead before morning. All you care about is my research. My guess is that you couldn't figure out my notes, which is why you dragged me here."

"Clever girl. Why did you write in code? Were you worried about your coworkers stealing your research?"

"No. There's no glory in Alzheimer's research. I created it in code because it kept my brain sharp. Having to decode the notes made my brain work harder to find the answers."

Miles chuckled, impressed and pleased, though it rankled that she'd put that look on his face. "You are going to do great things. I can only imagine the possibilities that could come from your brain."

"I won't help you," she said bluntly. "Unlike you, my morals and ethics are still firmly intact. Besides, MCX-209 had unintended consequences. Some of the monkeys tested had a complete memory wipe. They couldn't even remember how to eat a banana whereas some of the monkeys only had mild memory loss. The drug is unpredictable."

"A brilliant mind like yours needs only the room to figure out the kinks. I have complete faith in you."

"I don't think you're understanding what I'm saying—the drug isn't safe. It isn't safe for *monkeys,* much less humans. It would be unethical to release this drug into the general population."

"Absolutely. I completely agree. The general public has no need for such a drug and besides, it would never pass FDA approval, but there are people in power who would pay handsomely for a drug like this."

Kat felt the blood drain from her face. She hated

being right. "You're making a huge mistake. A drug like this is worse than anthrax. You can't sell it."

Miles smiled—a perfect example of how such a handsome face could hide such evil—and said, "My dear, Dr. Odgers…it's already a done deal, which is why you can understand why it's imperative that you fix what I've promised to deliver. I have certain contacts who would be willing to pay an arm and a leg for something such as your drug, but they also wouldn't bat an eye about tearing either one of us limb from limb if we renege."

She swallowed. "Maybe you shouldn't have made promises before you knew you could deliver. You might've screwed us both with your greed."

"As I said, I have faith in you. You will figure it out. The formula was so close. All you need is a quiet environment, your tools and the right motivation."

"I had all those things the first time and I failed. What makes you think anything will be different the second time around?"

"Because your life is at stake this time around and something tells me you have no wish to die a messy, painful death."

Well, he was right about that, but she didn't know if she could live with herself if she succeeded in creating the world's most dangerous drug.

Miles sensed her consternation and seemed to enjoy it. "This is the spice of life, our choices. We don't have to be enemies. I respect your talent and intelligence.

I find brilliant people very stimulating." He shocked her when he gave her a short, more assessing gaze that bordered on interested and she drew back with a scowl. "What? Although you lack the particular attributes I find attractive, I find your intellect arousing to a certain degree. You should be flattered."

"Go screw yourself," she retorted, feeling the need for a shower after being eye-raped by a man old enough to be her grandfather. "You're not my type. *At all.*"

"Fair enough," Miles said, shrugging off her insult and returning to their original topic. "The applications are endless and I'm eager to provide our buyers with the opportunity to test it out."

Fresh dread replaced her lingering revulsion. "You can't do that. It's illegal!" she protested, feeling much like a mouse caught in a trap. "I'll tell the police. I'll tell the media. I'll tell everyone I come into contact with."

"Pipe down for a moment and listen to reason. I am willing to offer you a cut. I could set you up with millions in exchange for your help in perfecting the formula. I've seen your apartment. Not much to brag about. I know your feebleminded uncle is languishing in a state-run facility, drooling into his pudding most days. Wouldn't you like to see him spending the rest of his days in comfort?"

Her eyes stung and she wanted to scream at him, *Don't you dare talk about my uncle!,* but her lips refused to move. She was paralyzed by the horror of the nightmare she was living in.

"You need time to process," he said with understanding. "It's a lot to take in and you've been through a terrible ordeal. I can give you the day to relax. Would you like a massage? A facial? Perhaps a pedicure? I can have that arranged for you. You are our guest, not a prisoner—at least not yet."

"Not yet?" she repeated numbly. "What does that mean?"

"It means if you're not of a mind to be helpful, I will no longer be of a mind to be a gracious host. I will have your cooperation, willingly or not."

"You can't make me do anything," she said. "I have nothing to lose. As you already stated, my one remaining family doesn't even realize I'm alive, so what do I have to lose? You can't make me. I won't help you. This drug could ruin lives and I don't care how much money you wave under my nose…I'm not budging."

Miles held her gaze as his narrowed and he pulled himself straight in his chair with a sigh. "What a pity. I was hoping for a good relationship between us. Camille, take Dr. Odgers to her room, please."

Camille appeared at Kat's side and grabbed her arm with a hard pinch, causing Kat to bite back a yelp. She skewered Camille with a dark look, which went unnoticed by Camille as she practically dragged her back to that tiny cell of a room.

"For a genius, you aren't very smart, are you?" Camille said with a smirk. "You think you can wait Miles out? He'll find your weak spot and then he'll dig both thumbs into it without mercy. Do yourself a favor and agree to help."

No one asked for your advice. "Where's Jake? Does he know about this?"

Camille checked her watch. "By this time, Jake Isaacs is likely dead. He was a loose end that Miles couldn't afford to let swing in the wind. Pity that. He was wonderful in bed." Kat reared back as if she'd been slapped and Camille laughed. "Oh, you poor thing. Were you seduced by his hard exterior and sad story? Don't feel bad. He's reeled in more than one pretty face with that story. Although in your case, he must've made an exception to the pretty face. Consider yourself lucky. He died before he could break your heart."

Camille's laughter followed her out the door. As soon as Kat was alone, she pulled her knees to her chest and buried her face against her kneecaps. It was all a lie. Everything. Jake had used her. Having confirmation was more painful than the wondering had been.

But even worse than the knowledge that she'd been used was the possibility that Jake was dead. Fresh pain skated across her heart and she sobbed hard.

She cursed the day she'd created that drug.

She cursed the day Jake Isaacs stormed into her life.

And she cursed her stupid, broken heart.

Chapter 18

Jake drove hard to Los Angeles, needing to get to Nathan's place as soon as possible. He wasn't sure where to start and he was afraid to make the wrong move, but each second that passed felt like the graze of a blade against his nerves. The old Camaro ate up the miles admirably and he supposed for as many times as he had to stop for gas, he was still making good time. But he only had cash to work with because he was certain now any credit card would've been tracked and he couldn't take the risk.

He should've listened to his gut because it'd never steered him wrong. His intuition had kept him alive over the years. Why he'd decided to ignore it this time was beyond him. No, that wasn't entirely true; he knew why'd he'd ignored it, because there were feelings involved—feelings he shouldn't have for Kat. Maybe he'd thought if he pushed her away the feelings would stop but now he was driven by a near insane pressure to fix what he had broken. The question was, could he? He'd done something terrible to Kat—taken something precious from her and given her pain and heartache in return. Kat could call him every name in the book if it meant that he could save her.

By the time he reached Nathan's house, it was dark and late. He went around the back so as not to attract attention and rapped on the sliding-glass door. Nathan's girlfriend, Jaci Williams, appeared, her eyes widening with surprise when she saw him. She opened the door and gestured for him to come inside. "What are you doing here, Jake? Is everything okay? Nathan told me that there was something going on but he didn't go into detail."

"I wish I could say everything was okay. But everything's pretty much fallen to shit. Where's Nathan?"

"He's in the garage, tinkering with his latest project. I'll go get him. Are you thirsty or hungry? I just put away the dinner stuff. I could fix you something really fast."

His stomach growled. "I could eat. Thanks. I've been eating MREs for so long I've forgotten what real food tastes like."

Jaci smiled and began pulling items from the refrigerator. "While I'm doing this why don't you go to the garage and get Nathan. I'll let you know when it's ready."

Jake smiled and nodded in appreciation. His mouth was already watering. "You're a doll, Jaci. Thank you."

Jake went into the garage through the small hallway near the laundry room and found Nathan working on an engine. Nathan looked up and frowned when he saw Jake. "Well, if you're here it must mean that things are pretty bad. What happened?" he said, going straight to the point. "Where is your target? The scientist?"

"She's in custody but I think that's the problem. I think there's a rat in the department."

"And what makes you think that?"

"The agent who tried to put a bullet in my gut during this bogus paperwork drop."

Nathan whistled. "Yeah that would've tipped me off, too. So start from the beginning and don't edit—I need to know everything if I'm going to help you."

Asking for help ground against Jake's every raw nerve but there was more at stake than just his pride— Kat's life might be in the balance and he'd sacrifice anything for her safety. "Kat created a drug—a real bad one—by accident. She was trying to create a drug to help Alzheimer's patients. The drug was supposed to help heal the damage done by the disease and restore memory but, in fact, it does the opposite. MCX-209 wipes the brain clean without any damage."

Nathan stared, almost uncomprehending. "Are you

kidding me? That's a seriously bad drug. In the wrong hands…this could be monstrous."

Jake nodded. "Yeah, I know. That's why the Defense Intelligence Department thought it would be best to bring her in for her own safety. It was my assumption that we would bring her into custody and debrief her to explain how she would have to change her life, take on a new identity and never go into science again in order to save her life, but once I turned her over I got a real bad feeling about how things were going to go down. And then it was something that the agent said that tipped me off. She called Kat a 'national treasure,' which didn't seem right. I should've listened to my gut. Because about an hour later someone was trying to take me out."

Nathan scratched an itch on his head with dirty fingers, oblivious. Jake knew Nathan was thinking about the ramifications. He didn't blame him. It was mind-blowing information. "So you think someone within your organization is going to sell her research for money?"

Jake shrugged but it was a good theory. "I don't know but it's possible. Corrupt governments would pay lots of money for this kind of drug. It would change the way wars are fought and won."

"Damn straight it would. Your girl is in a heap of trouble if it's true."

Jake stiffened. "She's not my girl. But I feel responsible for her. It's my fault she's in the wrong hands. I handed her over in spite of my misgivings." Jake ignored the sizzle of pain when he pictured Kat's crest-fallen expression when she discovered his betrayal. He couldn't think about that right now. He had to focus on what he could do to save her. "I need to know what contacts you have that can help me. I don't know what else to do."

Nathan grabbed a rag and wiped his hands. "Well, first let's get you some food. You look like hell. Let me guess, you've been eating MREs morning, noon and night."

"They're perfect fuel," was all Jake needed to say. "But I have to admit I'm ready to eat something else. Jaci's cooking me up some leftovers."

"Well, you are in luck. We had tacos, your favorite."

Jake scowled, hating any reference of their shared childhood. "Yeah, I guess," he muttered. "So who do you have who can help me?"

"What I think we need to do first is find out if there's been any intel put out on you. Chances are whoever put the hit on you has already discovered that you got away. So that means you're a loose cannon that they're gonna want to get under control right away. I wouldn't be surprised if they've declared you rogue by now. The best way to deflect attention from themselves is to put it on someone else. And you're a perfect target."

"Do you think you can nose around and find that information out? We're pretty tight with our security."

"No government agency is immune to security breaches if someone truly wants to find information.

Let me ask around first and if that doesn't yield any results I'll put James on the job. That man can hack into anything, including the DID."

Jake wasn't sure of that. Their security was second to none but at this point he was desperate. If Nathan thought Jaci's friend James could unlock some doors, then so be it. He was more than willing to try.

"Now tell me what's the real story about your scientist. What's really going on between you two?"

Jake stared at his brother, caught between the urge to lie through his teeth and confess his sins. "I promised her she would be safe. I never go back on my word." Except that he had. He had bald-faced lied to her and he didn't know if he could live with that. It felt like a knife stabbing him in the heart each time he replayed the conversation with her. He was haunted by her wide, vulnerable stare and later the way her lip trembled when she realized the truth. He was such a bastard. *I'll make it up to you, I promise. Just stay alive. Be smart.* "She didn't deserve any of this. She was just trying to make the world a better place. It's not her fault that a lab mistake has completely derailed her life."

"Little brother, you and I both know that life isn't fair. You care for this woman. I can see it all over your face."

Jake turned his gaze away from his brother, not trusting his ability to shutter his true feelings. "Nathan, don't make me regret coming to you for help. I feel responsible for her safety. Let's leave it at that."

Nathan sighed and rose from his perch. "You're such a prickly cuss. I remember you being a lot nicer."

"Yeah, well, things change."

Nathan didn't respond and simply exited the garage with Jake following. Yeah, he used to be a lot nicer. But their father had kicked that quality right out of him. And Jake didn't know if he'd ever get it back.

The following day Kat was ready to climb the walls of her small room when Camille returned to retrieve her. "I hope you're feeling more cooperative today. We have something to show you that you might enjoy."

"Is it a one-way ticket out of this terrible place?" she asked.

"No. But I think you'll like it."

"You wouldn't know what I like," she muttered, but followed Camille from the room, just happy to be free from those four walls.

They walked down a long, brightly lit hallway made of dense cement. The quality of the air suggested they were underground. Of course, that made perfect sense. But she had to be honest, she thought only movies featured underground bunkers where nefarious government experiments took place. It was pretty frightening to realize that it was possibly true. She'd never been a conspiracy theorist, more content to spend her time in her lab than wondering what terrible things the government was cooking up. Right about now she wished she'd been paying more attention to the world around her.

Camille punched in a code at an access point and the door slid open to reveal a state-of-the-art lab. The scientist in her leaped with joy at the familiar surroundings but her happiness was immediately cut short when she realized its purpose. They wanted her to make more MCX-209, in spite of the dangers she'd already explained. Miles appeared with a generous smile on his face as if he were providing her the lab out of the kindness of his heart. "What do you think? As good or perhaps better than what you had at Tessara?" The pride in his voice was unmistakable.

"I told you I'm not going to work for you. I don't care how nice the lab is. I have an *ethical* dilemma—get it?"

Miles surprised her when he nodded with complete understanding. "Yes, I understand your dilemma. And I want to help you get past that. I feel the best motivation is the one that comes from the heart." Miles looked to Camille and nodded. Camille disappeared and Miles kept talking. "You see I appreciate your brilliant mind. I was astounded by your research and by how fearless you were with your formulas. Every once in a while there comes along a brilliant mind operating under the radar and it's always been my dream to cultivate and foster that brilliance. Over the years I've had my minor successes but you, Dr. Odgers, are a shining gem with that incredible mind of yours. I'm honored to help facilitate the making of history with you."

"Are you insane? I told you I'm not going to help you. You have nothing that could compel me to help you create more of this awful drug. I have nothing that you can hold against me, nothing that I hold dear enough that you could use for leverage."

"It pains me to do this. But sometimes a little force is needed to make change happen. I take that responsibility seriously." Camille reappeared but this time she pushed a wheelchair and in the wheelchair sat her beloved uncle Chuck. Kat gasped in horror, stunned that they would sink so low. Her uncle, his mind long since disintegrated from the effects of the disease, stared off into space, unknowing and unseeing.

Camille patted Uncle Chuck's head as if he were an animal and Kat felt a growl rumble from her chest.

"You see, leverage can be found if only one looks hard enough."

"You're a bastard. How dare you kidnap my uncle like this? He needs medical care. Can't you see that he's not well?" she cried. "He'll die without medical intervention."

Camille smoothed the remaining hair on Uncle Chuck's head, causing Kat to seethe with rage. "We'll see to it that he is comfortable and well taken care of as long as you do as you're told," Camille said, pressing a small kiss on Uncle Chuck's cheek. "But if you continue to be difficult, I imagine Uncle Chuck might suffer."

Kat clenched her fists, wanting to bury each one of them in Camille's beautiful, perfect face. She pictured blood spurting and spilling all over her impeccable pantsuit, ruining the expensive fabric and causing Camille to shriek like a banshee.

Miles laughed at her rage. "Such a little spitfire. You'd better watch out, Camille. She has murder in her eyes," he said. "I think we've made our point. Go ahead and put poor Uncle Chuck back to bed. He looks tuckered out."

Camille nodded and wheeled Uncle Chuck from the room, leaving Miles and Kat alone again. "You see, it's not so hard to find someone's leverage. And I don't want to be the bad guy in this. In fact, you can still continue your work—good work—as long as you perfect MCX-209 for my purposes. I have a buyer who is very interested in obtaining a batch and the clock is ticking. What else do you need? I've obtained your notes and provided the necessary chemicals but I confess, I'm no scientist. So if there's anything I overlooked, please let me know and I will get it for you immediately."

Kat's eyes burned with tears she refused to shed. Her gaze wandered around the impeccably clean lab, every surface gleaming and new, and she knew she didn't have a choice. Her voice was choked with tears as she said, "I need monkeys. I need something to test the drug on."

"I'll do you one better," Miles said with a wink. "We have human subjects just waiting to test out your next batch."

Kat shook her head in horror, whispering, "No... no...please, don't make me do this." Humans? She couldn't bear the thought of destroying someone's brain with her drug like he wanted her to. "It's not right."

"Darling, ethics have no play here. I'm only interested in results. I've found you some human subjects. When can the first batch be ready?"

"I need three days and that's working around the clock," she said, her voice barely above a whisper.

"Excellent. I'll have your meals brought to you. I look forward to seeing your results in action. Oh, is there anything you prefer mealwise? We have culinary chefs at our disposal. Name your poison."

Kat's eyes watered and shimmered and only one thing came to mind. "Cookies and juice," she whispered, her throat clogging with tears.

"Very good." Miles smiled and turned to leave, but then stopped and regarded Kat with a warning in his eyes. "Don't think you can escape. As you might have surmised, we are several stories underground. This is a top-secret military facility and there are very few who know its location. I could keep you here for the rest of your life and no one would know. Do the right thing and do as you're told and this will all end well. Try to thwart me and I will destroy you and everyone you've ever come into contact with. Starting with your uncle—although to look at him a quick death might be a blessing, wouldn't you say?"

"Don't you have someone to answer to?" she asked, almost desperately. Kat couldn't imagine that everyone in this horrid place answered to Miles Jogan and his henchwoman Camille. Wasn't there anyone here who could help her?

"Everyone answers to someone, my dear. But here, I am king. My superior isn't even aware that this place is operational. One of the benefits of being a covert branch of the government, even the secret-keepers have secrets. So, before you start formulating a plan to plead your case to anyone who might listen, save your breath. There is no one here who would risk standing in my way. My reach is long—thanks to an esteemed military career—and I would crush anyone who dared to disobey an order down here. Understand that anyone who you could compel to help you, would be signing their own death warrant. Their blood would be on your hands."

"You're a manipulative bastard without a heart," she threw at him, knowing her insult would bounce right off him but she didn't care. "I hope you rot in hell for what you're doing to people. Someday karma will call in its chips and you're going to pay for the wicked things you've done in your life."

"I don't believe in karma. I believe in reality. You might try it sometime. Clock is ticking," he reminded her as he laughed at her tears and left her wishing she could chuck every sharp object within her grasp in his direction but she did nothing. She stood rooted to the spot, staring until he had left the room, leaving her behind to make the world's worst drug for his own purposes.

"Jake...I wish you were here. I don't know what to do."

In the end she didn't really think she could refuse Miles's demand and so she got to work.

Chapter 19

Jake knew bad news was coming just by the look on his brother's face. "I've been declared public enemy number one, haven't I?" At Nathan's slow nod, Jake cursed. "Well, isn't that a nice thank-you for all the years of service I've given. What did you find out?"

Nathan leaned forward and pushed a piece of paper toward Jake. "This is what I could find out by nosing around. You've been deemed armed and dangerous, priority one. Every single bounty hunter and government agent with their eye on a promotion is going to be gunning for you. Do you have any friends on the inside? Because you're going to need them."

Jake thought hard, running down a list of contacts in his mind. The problem was, Jake wasn't much of a friend-maker. He preferred handling things on his own, being beholden to no one. He could see now how having a few friends would've been an advantage. "Not really," he admitted sourly. "I didn't much see the value in cultivating friendships. Particularly in the work arena. It's not like I was going to invite them out for a beer or something."

"I understand. I was the same way. Guys like us, with a background like ours, just don't lend themselves to easygoing relationships—either in the friend department or the other. So we're going to have to come at this from the standpoint that you're completely alone. I've got a few friends I trust that I can contact."

"Yeah? Like who? I'm not sure we should be bringing in every Tom, Dick and Harry you've ever played poker with. A wrong move could get Kat killed."

"Cut me some slack," Nathan said with a touch of irritation. "As if I'd bring in anyone I couldn't trust implicitly. Now settle down and stop being such an ornery cuss. I'm trying to help you."

Jake bit down on his tongue, knowing his brother was right but he was having a difficult time remaining calm when he knew Kat was in danger— Even worse, that he was the one who put her there. He was supposed to keep her safe, not deliver her like a Christmas present to the enemy. "Who's your friend?" he asked, relenting.

"Remember my buddy Miko?" At Jake's nod, he said, "Well, I think his brother, Holden, can help us out."

At that Jake frowned. "The corrupt guy from ID? That's no glowing endorsement," he said. "How am I supposed to trust his brother when Miko was up to his eyeballs in corruption. For crying out loud, Nathan… Miko killed himself out of guilt. How is his brother going to help us?"

"Miko was a good guy—the best—but he got caught up in some bad shit. Got in way too deep and couldn't find his way out. That's got nothing to do with his twin brother, Holden. He's solid. Trust me."

"I don't know." Jake wasn't sure. Bringing too many people in could get complicated. "What can Holden do that we're not doing already?" he asked.

"Holden is a security and weapon specialist. He can get us the best weapons the military has to offer as well as help us get past the Zephyr system."

"James said the security system was the best in the business," Jake reminded his brother. "What can Holden do that James can't?"

"Totally different skill set. James is all about the computer stuff. Holden knows the actual hardware."

Jake grunted his acknowledgment but he wasn't keen on bringing in more people. More people meant more opportunity for information leaks. "I don't like it. I'd rather keep the information contained to this room with everyone on a need-to-know basis."

"You don't trust my judgment?"

"Don't go there. Kat is what matters right now and I'm not willing to take any chances. Let's leave it at that."

Nathan exhaled and pinched the bridge of his nose. "Fine. In the meantime you're going to need to lay low."

"There's no way that's going to happen. Every second that goes by that Kat isn't with me is a second that she's in danger. I can't live with that."

"Yeah, but if you don't think smart you're going to end up dead and how's that going to help your scientist?"

Jake hated the logic in Nathan's statement but it was true. He needed to think smart. Kat was counting on him. Even if she didn't know it. As far as she knew he'd abandoned and betrayed her. "So what am I supposed to do? Sit here and twiddle my thumbs? I have to do something. Put yourself in my place. If Jaci were in danger would you sit back and just wait for things to unfold?"

Nathan shook his head. "Hell, no. But I'm also the one known for being impulsive—you were the cool head."

"Yeah, well, I don't feel very coolheaded right now. I feel ready to rip someone's head off."

Nathan chuckled and Jake shot him a sharp look. "Hey, I'm just saying I know how you feel. When Jaci's life was threatened I was like a bear, and anyone who got in my way was gonna get torn apart. That's love for you. It changes you."

"Don't get ahead of yourself. I never said I was in love with Kat."

"You didn't have to. I can see it all over you. Listen, you can hide your feelings from everyone else but you can't hide them from me. We have issues, little brother, but I know you better than anyone in this world. Just admit it, you love her. It's okay, your secret is safe with me. And here's a news flash that took a long time for me to get…being in love doesn't make you weak. In fact, it makes you stronger."

Jake shifted with discomfort. "I don't love her…I just feel responsible for her. There's things you don't know…because it's none of your damn business but, hell, I don't know what I'm saying anymore. I ought to just keep my damn mouth shut."

Nathan surprised Jake by clapping him on the shoulder. "I spent a long time trying to convince myself that I didn't love Jaci. And it was miserable. Do yourself a favor and just admit it. Once you do you'll be a whole lot happier."

"I don't know how I feel about Kat. She's unlike anyone I've ever met. I'm intrigued by the way she looks at the world and how she makes me feel when I'm around her. I've been in love before and it didn't feel like this. She drives me crazy, honestly. Sometimes she's a real pain in the ass. But she has these brilliant green eyes that are almost mesmerizing and she thinks she's plain and homely, which is ridiculous because she's probably the most gorgeous woman I've ever laid eyes on. Particularly in the morning when she first wakes up." Jake realized he'd said too much but it was too late, his brother already knew so what information was he trying to protect? "I just need her back, Nathan."

"And we will do our best to get her back for you, Jakey," Nathan answered with all sincerity. Jake had a lot of issues with his brother—possibly problems they would never ever be able to resolve fully—but at that moment Jake was grateful for his brother's help and so he was willing to let his brother's use of his old nickname slide. At least this once.

"What's the first step? Give me a job, something I can do so I don't feel completely useless."

"Give me a list of your superiors and the chain of command. Who is your immediate supervisor?"

"Miles Jogan."

"That name sounds familiar," Nathan said. "Tell me about him."

"I don't know him well. He was recently promoted into the position from a different department. In fact, I think it was a lateral move, not an actual promotion, but he'd come with a long list of commendations. He's friends with the right people, that's for sure."

"Career military?"

"Yeah. Another army guy. Served in Desert Storm and a host of other skirmishes. Collected badges of honor along the way until he moved up the ladder. From there, he zigzagged around but he knew enough to take the positions that would put him in the right places for further advancement."

"Well, one thing is for sure, if he's involved with Tessara, chances are he's more than he seems. Each time that place pops up, trouble definitely follows. I wish the whole damn place would just fall to the ground, but not everyone shares my biased view."

Jake agreed. "I was surprised when Tessara didn't shut down when ID was shuttered due to their involvement with Penelope Winslow." Penelope Winslow was one of Tessara's owners, who turned out to be a money-grubbing sadist in her spare time, who was using ID as her personal killing force through the help of her lover—and Nathan's boss—Thomas Wyatt. It'd been a cluster-eff of royally screwed-up circumstances, the reverberations of which were still rocking certain circles.

"I think it's pretty safe to assume he's crooked, because he's the one who gave you the orders as well as facilitated the transfer and extraction of Dr. Odgers. But what about his boss? Can we trust him?"

"I've never had much dealing with *her* so I don't know. I don't know who to trust at this point. I don't have proof but I think Camille Stephens is working with Miles Jogan. I did recall a rumor floating around the office that those two were shacking up. If so, that would make sense of why she's working with him."

"So we need to find out if Miles's boss is crooked, too. And in the meantime we need to find where Miles would take Dr. Odgers. Do you have any ideas?"

"Yeah, actually I do. There's a top-secret military facility in New Mexico—sort of like Area 51—where Miles would have access to lablike facilities. He's high enough in the chain of command that he could conceivably take over an area in the lab without anyone lifting an eyebrow."

Nathan frowned. "I don't know of any top-secret military facility in New Mexico. Why don't I know about this?"

Jake smirked. "Different department. The DID does some interesting experiments, ones that explore the power of the brain, and it's easier to hide underground what you're doing rather than a building that can be picked up by Google Earth. Let's just say the press are not invited for tours of this facility."

"Okay, so how tight is the security?"

"Tighter than Fort Knox. It'll be downright impossible to get into that facility."

"Nothing's impossible. I learned that after my ordeal with ID. We just have to figure out what we need and then procure it. I'll get James to master the security system and in the meantime we need to figure out if Miles's superior knows what he's up to. Something tells me Miles is the one who's gone rogue but no one knows it yet."

"Miles's superior is a real ballbuster from what I hear, but I can't imagine that she's part of this. She's a real stickler for the rules. Her name is Michelle Rainier. She's former army, also highly ranked."

"Good. So we'll tap in to her emails, nose around and see if she has anything that might seem suspicious. If she seems clean we'll make contact."

"I wish there was a way to get ahold of Kat to let her know that she's not alone."

"I know, buddy. Hang in there. We'll get her."

Jake heard the promise in his brother's voice and for some reason it bolstered his flagging spirit. He shouldn't be so dependent upon his older brother—he was an adult for crying out loud and a soldier just the same as Nathan—but it felt good to know that Nathan had his back.

"Just for the sake of argument, how soon did you know that you were in love with Jaci?"

Nathan sobered. "I know a lot of people say love at first sight doesn't exist—that it's all horseshit—but they're wrong. I knew when I saw her she was different. It hit me like a thunderbolt. There was no one like her in the world and there never will be. Maybe that's not how it works for everyone but that's how it worked for me. And if I was confused at first and not willing to believe it, all of that went away the first time I kissed her. She tasted like *mine*. That's how I knew."

Jake quieted, not trusting what might fall from his mouth. What Nathan had described was exactly how he felt about Kat. *She tasted like mine.* Kat Odgers was meant for him, even if neither one of them had seen it coming. But what to do about it? He supposed he'd figure that out later. First he had to save her ass—and his own.

Camille traced a lazy circle on Miles's chest as they basked in the afterglow of their afternoon nookie session. Camille was an animal in bed and often he needed a moment to recoup. This was his favorite type of quiet time, with the sweat drying on their bodies and their thoughts resting after the explosion of their mutual satisfaction. But today, Camille wasn't content to simply enjoy the moment as he was. "So how many buyers are lined up now?" she asked. "When can we start the bidding process?"

"So impatient, my love. The word has already spread and there are many people interested in our little formula. If I were an ethical man I would say we should sell the formula to the most responsible person but thankfully my ethics can be persuaded by the top dollar."

Camille giggled, the little girl sound directly at odds with the hard, military persona. "I want a yacht. I've always wanted a yacht with a personal chef. That sounds so extravagant."

"Then you shall have one. When this deal is closed you will have your heart's desire."

Camille sobered, drawing attention to the dangerous game they played. "If we're caught...our lives will be over."

At that Miles laughed. "My dear, if we're caught we'll have no life to worry over. We will be killed. The stakes are very high. You knew that when you went in on this with me."

"I know. Jake is still out there. What can we do about him? He's a loose end we can't afford."

Miles knew that. The dilemma of Jake Isaacs plagued

him every night, though it wouldn't help to have Camille worrying about it, too. "I've got the situation with Jake under control. As far as everyone else is concerned, he's gone rogue. Someone will see him and bring him in. I have a plan for good ol' Jake."

"Are you going to tell me this plan?"

"And ruin the surprise? Of course not. You'll just have to wait."

"It makes me nervous having him out there. He has the power to take us down. And I don't like that. I don't like being threatened."

"I would never let anything happen to you. Trust me when I say that everything is going to plan."

"And what about Dr. Odgers? What happens to her when she's finished making the last batch of MCX-209?"

"Another regrettable loose end."

"Won't it be hard to make her disappear? Someone at Tessara Pharm is likely to notice she's missing eventually."

"As far as Tessara is concerned, she left for greener pastures. I have someone on the inside of Tessara. And they've already submitted her resignation paperwork."

"You think of everything, don't you?" Camille asked, a coy smile wreathing her lips. "I knew there was a reason why I found you insanely attractive."

"And here I thought it was only my good looks."

"Well, those don't hurt." Camille climbed on top of

Miles, giving him a glorious view of her full breasts and tight body. "So where did you get the test subjects?"

"Homeless people with little to no family to care about them. Offer them three squares a day, a bed and the promise of a little pocket change, and they're willing participants."

"Brilliant," Camille said, approving. "And if the initial tests don't go well?"

"No one will miss them," Miles said. "And besides, I'm doing the city a favor by thinning the herd of homeless."

"Yeah, well, the liberals might not feel the same."

"Yes, well, I'm not asking for their opinion." Miles reached up to cup her breasts. "Enough about that business. I'm far more interested in round two."

"Feeling frisky today?" she purred, rubbing against him in the way she knew drove him mad. "Are you sure?"

He answered by driving himself into her, effectively shutting her up.

Sometimes Camille talked way too much.

Chapter 20

Kat's hands shook as she removed her sample and prepared the syringe. *Please don't make me do this. Please don't make me do this*—that was the plea running through her head, but she knew no one was going to come save her and prevent the monstrosity that was going to happen. It was one thing to experiment on monkeys; they were cute but ultimately animals, a step below human beings. And while at times she felt a twinge of regret for a failed experiment that had undesirable side effects on the animal, she was always thankful that a human hadn't undergone testing. But not this time. This time her test subjects were human and she wanted to barf.

Miles Jogan appeared, the hated devil himself, wearing a satisfied and very smug smile. What she wouldn't give to rip out his nostril hairs one by one. "I've heard you were ahead of schedule," he said, pleased. "I knew you were a good investment."

"I don't think this is a wise decision," she said, trying for reason. "The formula is unstable and the effects are inconsistent. I really have no idea what it's going to do at any given time."

"Well, we can't have that. We need a stable formula, so figure it out. You're a smart one. I have faith in you."

"If I knew how to fix it, I would have prevented this from happening in the first place. I don't know where I went wrong," she said, her voice rising. She was operating on forty-eight hours without much sleep and even less food. Unless cookies counted as food. "You're making a terrible mistake. You don't have the right to mess with people's lives like this. This is so wrong on so many levels…" She stopped in midsentence because she knew her words were wasted and she had little energy to spare. Her shoulders drooped as she tapped the syringe and squeezed out the air. "Bring me the first subject," she instructed dully, just wanting this nightmare to be over already.

"There's my girl," Miles said, beaming. He gestured and Camille ushered in an older gentleman with a frizz of white hair and a weathered face. He shuffled in, eyes darting from side to side, clearly confused as to where he was or what was happening and Kat's heart broke for him. Was he someone's father? Was he someone's beloved uncle? They'd never know, at least not after she poked him with her syringe. Miles addressed the older man. "Hello, sir, what's your name?"

"Adam," the man answered. "I was told I could have a drink." His eyes shifted, clearly discomfited by the lab setting. She didn't blame him. If he had the sense God gave a goose, he'd run screaming in the other direction. But she could see how his hands shook, likely caused by years' worth of alcohol addiction, and her hopes sank. This man could no more recognize danger than a baby. A perfect victim—a perfect subject.

"Yes, yes, you will get your drink. Are you a Scotch man? As soon as you get your injection you can have your drink." He gestured to Kat. "Dr. Odgers, if you please?"

Kat approached Adam nervously. "This might pinch a little," she said, wanting to add "this might turn you into a quivering ball of Jell-O" but she didn't dare. Whispering a tiny prayer, she administered the drug. When Adam didn't immediately fall to the floor convulsing, she exhaled a small, relieved breath. "How do you feel?"

"I feel okay. Do I get my drink now?"

Kat nodded, although she didn't have a clue whether a drink was coming his way but she wanted to offer this man something for the cost of his compliance. She had no idea how Miles managed to get his test subjects but Kat suspected honesty had not been part of it. She looked to Miles and said, "Please get this man his drink."

Miles nodded slowly, his gaze narrowing at the test subject as if watching for any immediate adverse effects. "Of course. How soon will we know the drug has taken effect?"

"With Auguste, it took eighteen hours. I don't know if it will happen sooner or later with a human subject," she said, adding with a glare. "There's a reason we don't test on humans."

"Well, we'll just have to see what the next eighteen hours brings. Camille, could you please escort this gentleman back to his room? Oh, and get the man a Scotch. I think he may have earned it."

Camille took Adam away and Kat sat heavily on her stool, still shaking. "You're an evil man. You're the kind of person who can stab another in the back while smiling. Your soul is likely a shriveled-up husk by now."

Miles tsked. "That's not very nice. For someone as brilliant as you, you are very narrow-minded. Innovation, exploration and change always come at a cost. You are simply learning that lesson. I think you're missing the bigger point—and surprisingly, it has little to do with the money I'll earn from this venture. There are bigger applications, with a more humanitarian bent to this type of drug. Imagine if you could modify it to perhaps erase a terrible memory from a child? So that they wouldn't have to grow up with the stain of that one horrid event in their life. Wouldn't that be worth what we're doing today? I'm not a terrible man but I am a practical man. My pension will not support me and I have no wish to die at my desk. Working poor does not appeal to a person like me. I confess, I've become rather fond of tailored suits and those don't come cheap. Why should I continue to sacrifice my needs? I've done my duty, served my country and the best I can hope to gain is a worthless medal and a lousy pension with dwindling health care? No, I'm sorry. I've given too much to receive so little in return. I'm a man of action and I will have my compensation, one way or another."

"You don't have to eat off gold plates to live nicely," she said, glaring at his selfishness. "Most people would feel very fortunate to have a government pension like yours. It may not be millions but something tells me you wouldn't starve."

"That's not the point, is it? I have needs that unfortunately, the U.S. government's retirement plan does not fulfill. Rather than moan about it, I found ways to diversify my income. Is it so wrong that I don't wish to live in poverty?"

"You're a narcissist. You don't care about how this drug will affect the world. All you care about is how it affects you. Don't try to sell it to me as anything other than that."

He exhaled and shrugged as if he were caught. "Smart girl. You're right. I don't care about other people. I care about me. Start administering the sample in the other test subjects. We need to be able to compare results."

"Ruining one man's life should be enough until we figure out if it works. Don't you realize that this drug could literally disintegrate a person's brain? Don't you care? Wait, don't answer that, I know you don't care. But I find it hard to believe that you could be that bad of a person. Didn't you have parents, anyone who taught you right from wrong?"

Miles found her questioning amusing. "I will return in eighteen hours to check on Subject A. Word to the wise, Dr. Odgers. You're looking a little worn. Perhaps a short rest would do you wonders. Even a ten-minute nap can clear the mind of the cobwebs."

"A nap isn't going to make me feel better about what you're making me do," she snapped.

"Temper, temper." Miles tsked but his stare snapped with a warning. "I'd hate for poor Uncle Charlie to suffer on account of your stubbornness. Starving to death is a terrible way to go."

"Don't you dare hurt my uncle," she said, tears stinging her eyes. "I know you think you have all the cards right now but I swear to you, if you hurt him, I will go to my grave trying to find a way to kill you. No one is untouchable forever."

"You ought to turn all that passion toward your work— it'd be far more productive. Rest up, girl. You'll need it." He paused at the door. "And another thing, do us both a favor and stop trying to insert your morals and values into the current situation. They are neither appreciated nor appropriate and my patience has begun to wear thin."

Kat wanted to scream as Miles let himself out of the lab. His so-called concern for her welfare was a mockery. The bastard. But she was exhausted. Her eyes were crossing, and her stomach was cramping. Not enough sleep and too much sugar—a recipe for disaster. She groaned and stumbled to the small bathroom adjoining the lab. This was hell, she was pretty sure of it.

And Miles Jogan and Camille Stephens pinch-hit for the devil.

"You Isaacs boys really know how to piss people off," James said as he entered the room carrying his laptop. He paused to shake Jake's hand, a big grin on his face. "I gotta say, when one of you comes knocking I know I'll have one heck of a challenge—but I love a challenge. I've got information for you."

Jake allowed a relieved smile as James set up his laptop. James Cotton was a hacker in his free time and a blogger by day. Jake first met James a few months ago when all hell broke loose with Jaci and Nathan as ID imploded with wicked corruption. James had been Jaci's roommate for a time, which is why Nathan tolerated the man. It baffled him that a man could get paid just for writing stuff on the internet but James had made it lucrative. The blogging gig also gave him a pretty good cover for the hacking business that he did in his spare time. In fact, James was a bit of a nuisance on the internet, but he never tried to rip people off, so Jake gave him a pass. And thank God for that. Because he needed James's skills right now. "I'm happy to hear that. What do you got for me?"

"According to the information that Nathan gave me, I was able to bust into the Defense Intelligence Agency pretty easily. Your security is basic as far as government agencies go. I find that curious—do you think when this is all over I can get a side gig there as an IT guy? They sure as hell need one. Anyway, I was able to hack in to your boss's account and Miles Jogan doesn't leave a paper trail, if you know what I mean. Nothing in his email to suggest that he's up to no good. So that doesn't really help us. However, I did find quite a few cell phone text messages to Camille Stephens that suggest they're having a hot and heavy affair. I don't know what your policy is on interoffice dating but whoa! Some of those texts were downright disgusting." James stopped to give a lecherous grin and Jake had to smother a laugh even though he found the idea abhorrent. "Okay, now as to your big, big boss, her emails are equally clean and if she's involved she certainly isn't leaving a paper trail, either."

"So what do we do?"

"Well, aside from tapping their phone and recording some conversations, I don't know. But we have bigger problems." That got Jake's attention. "Here's the thing, while your internet security was really easy to breach, getting past your *actual* security in your building is going to be a bitch."

"I was afraid of that. That building was meant to withstand a nuclear bomb, an alien invasion and the zombie apocalypse."

"Yep. Pretty much. They're using a state-of-the-art security system created by Zephyr—best in the business. Voice recognition, laserbeam floor grid, encrypted phone lines…the list goes on and on. Honestly, dude, I don't know how you could break into this place unless you had Gandalf on your side."

Jake swore under his breath and leaned against his chair, closing his eyes as a headache began to pound against his temples. Nathan tried to console him. "We'll find a way," his brother said, but Jake knew there was no other way.

"There's no way we're sneaking into that building. Maybe if it wasn't underground…but this? Hell, we're so screwed."

James had to agree. "I'm sorry, man. I wish I had better news. I had thought that maybe if I could breach the security through the internet connections but…Zephyr is something else. They're the best. The only way you're getting into that building is if somebody wants you to get in. And I can't imagine that happening."

At that Jake perked up and sent a sharp look to Nathan. Nathan immediately began shaking his head. "No, man. Don't even think about it. That's a one-way ticket to dying."

"Not necessarily. Our biggest problem is getting in—not getting out."

"No. It's too big of a risk." Nathan was adamant against it. "I'm not letting my little brother walk to his death. There's gotta be a better way."

"There isn't. Besides, all I got to do is get in. Once I get in I can find Kat and then we can get out."

"And how do you think you'll manage that? You think that they'll just let you waltz in, grab your girl and walk out? The minute you show your face, you're on lockdown. Come on, you know this. You're not thinking with your head."

James jumped in. "Actually, he might be onto something. If he could get in I could show him how to introduce an infection into the mainframe, to disable Zephyr long enough for all systems to go down for a short time. Sort of like on *Jurassic Park* when the fat guy tried to steal the dino sperm in that fake can of shaving cream." He looked to Jake. "Do you know the layout of this building?" At Jake's nod, James continued excitedly. "Good. Then while everyone else is running around trying to figure out what's going wrong, you can swoop in and grab Kat and get out. It's perfect. Although, to be honest, you still have a snowball's chance in hell to make it work, but hey, what's life without a challenge, right?"

Nathan scowled at James, not appreciating his humor. "Watch it. You're talking about my brother's life. This is a high-stakes game. Any wrong move can get us all killed. Try to remember that."

"Hey, you asked me for my help. I didn't say that I would supply an airtight solution. That's all I got."

Nathan shook his head clearly unhappy with the solution. "We'll just have to think of something else," he insisted, but Jake was already moving forward.

"No, this is the way it has to be. They want me—they can have me. But I'm walking in packing. I'm going to need supplies. Do you think you could get me a few things?"

"Such as?" Nathan asked warily.

Jake grinned. "The fun stuff. The stuff ID specialized in—spy-cam pen, fake skin patch, stuff that will help me get out of that place alive."

Nathan nodded slowly. "Yeah, I can get you that stuff. I still think this is a risky idea. I don't like it."

"It's all we got. We have to make it work."

"Yeah, but I don't have to like it." Nathan scowled. He looked to James. "You think you can make a virus strong enough to take down the Zephyr system from the inside?"

"Hell, yeah. I've been working on something that could shut down most of Manhattan."

Jake looked at James. "Why do you create these viruses if you have no intentions of unleashing them?"

James shrugged. "I get bored."

Jake shook his head, not quite understanding a person like James but glad he was on their side. "You need a new hobby. I'll make contact with Miles and tell him that I'm coming in. He'll be more than happy to throw the doors open for me. With any luck he won't realize that I know he's up to his neck in corruption. In the meantime, Nathan, I need you to send some information to Miles's boss, detailing what we think we know. It'll be speculation and we have no proof but it will be enough to get her sniffing around. All we can do is pray that she's not on his side and just as corrupt."

Suddenly James chuckled and both Nathan and Jake turned to stare. "What's so funny?" Jake asked.

"I was just thinking how similar this is to the situation at ID. Like I said, you brothers have a knack for finding trouble. You don't find the humor? No? Huh. Guess it's just me, then."

It wasn't funny at all. Jake had long looked down his nose at Nathan's branch of the government, considering it a rogue organization that operated on the fringe of the law. To find out that the Defense Intelligence Department was no better made him a bit sick to his stomach. It also made him wonder if he'd been fighting on the wrong side all this time. He liked to think he was the good guy. But who knows?

Nathan must've known about his inner turmoil and shook his head for Jake's benefit, saying, "It's not the same. Your department is far more cerebral than ID ever was. We were the muscle, you were the brains. There's still good people inside of your department. Don't lose faith. Come on, let's focus on the important stuff, so we all don't get our asses killed."

Jake nodded, appreciating Nathan's support even as a twinge of guilt followed. "Thanks, man. I might not deserve your help but I'm glad I have it."

"There's nothing about deserving—we're brothers. I wasn't there for you when you needed me, and that eats me up inside. You have no idea the guilt I carry. I know it was bad for you when I left. I was a kid and I didn't know what to do. And I was being selfish. But I won't put my needs above yours again. You were counting on me then and I failed. I won't fail you this time."

Tears burned behind Jake's lids. He didn't know what to say. Thankfully James jumped in to defuse the moment. "Are you guys gonna hug or something? Geesh… I feel like I'm surrounded by a bunch of girls. Let's get a move on. We got a lot to do."

Jake and Nathan shared a smile. Nothing else needed to be said. James was right—it was time to move on.

Besides, what mattered most was saving Kat. They'd figure everything else out later.

Chapter 21

Kat awoke with a start, realizing she'd fallen asleep at the desk again. She plucked a Post-it note from her forehead and stared blearily around her lab. How many days had it been? The state of events had begun to blur. The first batch of MCX-209 had gone terribly wrong. And her mind was numb with the horror of it. She'd made minor modifications to the formula with disastrous results. At about twelve hours, the subjects had begun to convulse. And then their brains had turned into mushy pulp. When the guards found them, brain matter had been leaking from their ears. It was horrific—something out of a movie that Kat would've never paid to see. And yet here she was again, getting ready to administer another sample to a new round of subjects. Her own brain felt ready to break.

Kat shoved a cookie down her throat, mindlessly chewing for the sugar rush that was keeping her synapses snapping. The door slid open and a stranger walked in, pushing a cleaning cart. Her spirits fell when she realized it was the janitor.

Miles had already warned her that reaching out to anyone in this facility was a waste of time and dangerous to boot but she was nearing delirium and rational thought was slipping out of her grasp. "Can you help me?" she begged, sliding from her stool and walking toward the nervous-looking man as he avoided making eye contact. "Please? I'm a prisoner here! They're making me do terrible things to innocent people." When the man refused to answer and pushed his mop away from her, swabbing the floor quickly as if he were afraid she might jump on his back in an attempt to escape, she struggled to calm her rising hysteria and scratched out a quick note to thrust it at him with shaking fingers. "Please, take this note to the authorities. No one has to know that it was you. I'm going to lose my mind if they make me inject someone else with this drug."

At that, the janitor peeped a quick look at her, faint horror in his expression. "You the one who killed those people?"

"What?" Kat drew back but then realized the janitor might've been the one to clean up the gooey messes left behind. She swallowed and nodded numbly but hastened to explain. "They're making me do these things. I don't want to. I told them the formula was dangerous but they're forcing me to inject the subjects."

"I can't help you. Even if what you're saying is true," he mumbled, averting his gaze again. "Besides, how am I supposed to know if you're telling the truth? There's so many experiments going on in this damn place, it's hard to know who's talking straight because everything is so hush-hush. I keep my head down and do my work— that's how I stay employed."

And alive, Kat realized. New tears burned behind her lids. "What's your name?"

He looked reluctant to share but answered, "George."

"Nice to meet you, George. My name is Kat."

George nodded and began pushing his mop again but Kat had to ask him another question, one that she wasn't sure she wanted to know the answer to. "You're the janitor here? Are you the only janitor?"

"No, we have a night shift guy, too. Why?"

"They have my uncle here…I wondered if you'd seen him. He's…disabled."

George thought for a moment, then nodded slowly. "He's an older guy? Seems kinda lost in the head?"

Kat nodded, her heart squeezing. "Yes. He has Alzheimer's. Are they treating him well? Is he comfortable?"

Realizing she needed some kind of assurance, George nodded. "Yeah, they're treating him real good.

He's in a decent bed and gets good food. They even have a nurse check in on him."

She had no idea if George was feeding her a line of garbage but she accepted his answer in the hopes that it might be true. It was bad enough that she was stuck here, but doubly worse that they'd dragged her uncle Chuck into this horrid place, too. Her one saving grace was the knowledge that her uncle wasn't truly aware of his surroundings any longer. Unlike her, he didn't know that he was a prisoner because he was already a prisoner in his own mind. "Thank you, George," she said, wiping at her tears.

George seemed touched by her gratitude and added, "You need to eat more than cookies and juice. Gotta keep your strength up. Load up on more protein if you can."

"Thanks," she murmured, suddenly thankful for the human kindness even if he couldn't help her escape. "I'll try."

He nodded and pushed his cart out, leaving her alone again.

Kat returned to her stool and stared at her notes, wondering how to make the formula work. A part of her wondered if her subconscious was blocking her because she didn't want the formula to work at all. She remembered the first time she'd realized she was onto something amazing for Alzheimer's research. The thrill, the adrenaline rush, the potential had been seriously addicting. After that she'd worked tirelessly, almost giddily, too focused on the end game to consider the ramifications of a catastrophic failure. In some ways, she'd been just as single-mindedly determined as Miles to achieve her goal.

She wiped at the remaining moisture on her cheeks and wondered how her good intentions had managed to go so awry. Wasn't that the way of things? The saying "The road to hell is paved with good intentions" was certainly appropriate here. And speaking of hell…

The door slid open and Camille brought in the first subject of the day, this time a woman. Another drug addict. It broke her heart that no one would miss them, and Kat swore if she ever managed to get out of this place she would try to find their families to let them know what had happened. She didn't know how she would make that happen but she knew someone had to try. It wasn't right what Miles was doing, and it scared her that this was even happening. She was living in the world of Jason Bourne, and she'd never really been a fan of spy movies. Now she was starring in one.

"This is Anna," Camille said by way of introduction. Frankly, Kat found this little game a bit macabre. Camille seemed to enjoy it, though. "Anna is very eager to be part of this study. She has suffered from her addiction for a very long time. Haven't you, Anna?"

Anna, skin and bones from the waste of her addiction, nodded vigorously. "I'm willing to do anything to get off the drugs. I've suffered for so long. I've lost my family, I've left my job, I've left everything that ever meant anything to me. So if being part of this test study group helps me and helps other people beat this, I'm willing to do it. Maybe if I get better I can go see my kids again." She glanced shyly at Kat. "Do you got kids?"

"No," Kat murmured, unable to meet the woman's gaze, although she realized with a start that she could be pregnant at this very moment. She'd been so focused on seducing Jake because she'd been pretty sure she was going to die that she hadn't given much thought to contraception. The realization rattled her so much that she completely lost focus and nearly dropped the syringe. Camille's sharp voice brought her back to the present with jarring force.

"Doctor, are you all right?" Kat swung her gaze to Camille and jerked a short nod, not trusting her voice. She didn't regret her choice to sleep with Jake and there was nothing that could make her want to take it back. Even if it meant she'd gotten pregnant. The odds hadn't been in favor of conception because of the timing in relation to her cycle but that was no guarantee. What if one of Jake's swimmers was particularly industrious? She smiled in spite of the gravity of her situation because she could imagine that if Jake was hardheaded and stubborn, perhaps his sperm were, too.

Camille gestured to the woman with a look in her eyes that said, *get moving,* and Kat advanced toward the woman with resignation, though the woman didn't seem to notice her reluctance.

"That's too bad. You're young still, maybe someday. Before I got hooked on drugs, I was a good mom. I want to be a good mom again. Kids are good. They make life bearable. If I could do it all over again, I'd spend the rest of my life doing right by my girls," Anna said with the sort of bleak wistfulness that could wrench a tear from the most stoic. Except from Camille, because she'd been created by stone, apparently.

"That's very nice, Anna," Camille said with perfunctory politeness. "Would you mind rolling up your sleeve so the doctor can give you the injection?"

"I hope this works," Anna said, looking to Kat for reassurances.

The hope in Anna's eyes made Kat want to scream, *Run! You're going to die!* However, she could do nothing but smile wanly and say, "Thank you for volunteering," nearly choking on the words. She sent Camille a withering stare, which bounced off the woman with little consequence. "This might pinch a little." Kat administered the drug and felt a little piece of her soul die. Camille smiled and seemed the picture of kindness as she led the woman from the room.

This was the routine for the next four subjects—a scary little game where only Camille and Kat knew the stakes. After all five test subjects had been injected, Camille returned, much to Kat's chagrin. She'd much rather spend time with Miles if she had a choice, because when Camille spent time with Kat, she loved digging the knife in a little deeper about Jake, and with

Kat's current state of mind she was ready to smash a beaker over Camille's head.

"You look dreadful," Camille observed, her gaze trailing over the various instruments with a sense of detachment. "But then scientists like you, your looks aren't so important, are they? Sometimes I envy people like you—plain, homely, with no expectations of beauty. Sometimes it's such a burden to be as attractive as I am."

Oh, boo hoo. Was she freaking serious? Kat glared. "Did you have a purpose here or was it just to bug me?"

"I'm just curious—why you? Jake has never batted an eye during a mission. He's stoic, focused, a near-perfect soldier. Until you. You changed everything. And for the life of me I can't figure out why. You're skinny, you have no breasts and you sort of remind me of a mouse. It's baffling."

"Maybe he didn't like shallow people," Kat answered pointedly, her throat nearly closing on the wave of grief that followed. She couldn't talk about Jake. It hurt so much. She'd only known him a short time but her heart didn't seem to recognize that small fact. In her heart, she felt as if they'd known each other a lifetime. "Let me guess, you were a one-time fling? A one-and-done? Sucks to be cast aside, doesn't it?"

Camille's gaze narrowed. "Such a smart mouth to go with that genius brain."

Kat shrugged. What a screwed-up conversation. She hated the idea of Jake being intimate with this awful woman. Her pretty face hid a monster's soul. "Did you have a point?" Kat asked, done with this chat. It was bad enough knowing that Jake had betrayed her, but it was even worse knowing he was dead. She tried not to think about it, because the pain was crippling. "I have work to do. Don't you have a job aside from pestering me?"

"You really should work on your personality. Because that's all you have…well, I suppose you have your brains, too. At least for now."

With that little slip, Kat stilled. A chill chased her spine. "What is that supposed to mean?"

Camille covered her mouth as if she were shocked by her indiscretion but it was all an act. Kat knew Camille had dropped that information intentionally. "Let's just say you should have done a better job impressing Miles."

"And what would that have accomplished? I think the role of whore was already taken," she countered, and Camille's lip curled in a snarl.

"As if Miles would waste his time sniffing after someone like you. You're weak and pathetic. Your only value is resting precariously on the success of this formula."

"I guess that's probably true, but I wonder why Miles made a pass at me, then?" She pretended to ponder her own question, to what purpose she didn't know other than it felt good to get under Camille's skin, and then shrugged, saying, "But don't worry, I told him I wasn't interested. He's not really my type. I prefer men closer to my own age. Does he pop a Viagra before inviting you into his bed? If so, be careful. If he has a heart condition or high blood pressure, a drug like that could spell trouble for his ticker."

"Miles would never be interested in someone like you. What do you have to offer that I don't?" Camille sneered but there was a hint of insecurity behind her arrogance that Kat gleefully latched on to.

"What do I have to offer? Brains. He likes smart girls apparently. They turn him on. So if you don't turn his crank that way, it must mean, you're not his intellectual equal. Makes you wonder how long he's going to keep you around once he gets bored with what's between your legs."

Camille stiffened with rage but suddenly caught a hold of herself. Her self-restraint was admirable. Kat had been hoping she'd lose her marbles and start throwing stuff. Any hitch in Kat's ability to produce the formula was a win in her book.

"I wonder...did you use that sharp tongue of yours on Jake? Somehow I doubt it. You probably played the part of the poor, pathetic woman, clinging to Jake like a lemur. He always did like playing the hero. How does it feel to know that you're the reason he's dead?"

A quake started at the base of Kat's spine and she clenched her fists to prevent herself from grabbing the first object within reaching distance to hurl at Camille's smug face. "Get out of my lab. Or I'll tell Miles that you're impeding my progress. Somehow I don't think he'll appreciate that."

"Very well, then. I've bored of this conversation, anyway. Enjoy your remaining time…what little you have left of it." Camille's mouth widened in a cruel smile and she turned on her heel, leaving Kat's lab.

As soon as Camille was gone, Kat sagged. They were going to kill her as soon as she'd perfected the formula. If she weren't such a coward she would kill herself before completing the formula so that no one could have this terrible drug but she couldn't do that. Besides, her uncle Chuck was in this horrible building somewhere. And even if he didn't know where or who he was—she knew and there was no way she'd leave him here alone with the piranhas.

Was it almost a week ago that Jake was alive or was it two? Kat had lost track of time. Time didn't exist in this underground box. She didn't know if it was day or night. She didn't know if it was raining or cold or hot or balmy. She didn't even know where she was. All she knew was that she was a prisoner on death row and the clock was ticking. She wasn't going to get out of here alive, that much was true and inescapable. And not for the first time since waking up in this awful place, Kat felt tears sliding down her cheek.

Sometimes crying was the only thing you could do about a situation.

Jake dialed the code for Miles's office. The phone picked up on the first ring. "Miles! Thank God, I need to talk to you. Something bad is going down."

Jake purposefully put the urgency in his voice, hoping Miles bought that he was unaware of Miles's involvement. It worked.

"Jake! We've been so worried! Where are you?"

"A small hotel in the middle of nowhere. I'm trying to get to D.C. but someone's on my tail. Someone intercepted the last job packet and gave me bad information."

"Bad, how?"

"It was a setup. They tried to kill me."

"Forget D.C. Come straight to New Mexico to The Bunker. Do you know how to get here?"

"Yeah, I think so. Why the change?" he asked, making it seem as if he was confused.

"I think we have a mole in the department. I don't trust the D.C. office right now. Come here so we can debrief you. Did you get a description of the person who tried to gun you down?"

"No, not really," he lied. "It happened so fast. I barely got out with my life."

"Come straight away. Do you need a pickup? I can have a plane pick you up within the hour."

"That would be great. I'm exhausted."

"Come on home, Agent Isaacs. We'll get you rested up and right as rain in no time."

"Look forward to it, sir."

Miles gave Jake the coordinates where the private plane would touch down and then they signed off.

"Do you think he bought it?" Nathan asked.

"Yes. I don't think he suspects a thing."

"Good. You're going to need to get in and get out. The security failure will only be for five minutes. That's not a lot of time."

"I know."

"I'll be waiting with a car on the south side entrance, away from the video surveillance. I've already sent an email to Michelle Rainier. Hopefully, it works in our favor. If not, be prepared to disappear because this could get ugly for us all."

"If I don't come out in five minutes, I want you to leave," Jake told his brother. "I mean it. Don't hang around. If I'm not out in five, that means something went wrong. You hear me?"

"You know it's pointless to ask me to leave you behind. Just do your best to get your ass out in a timely manner so I don't have to go in after your sorry behind."

"I mean it, Nathan. I don't want you caught up in this any more than you already are."

"And I mean it, too. You're my brother. You don't come out—I'm going in. End of story."

Jake swore under his breath but even as he wished his brother would stop being so stubborn, he swelled with pride that such a man had his back. "Fine. It's your funeral," he grumbled, and Nathan laughed.

"If I don't come back, it's *your* funeral because Jaci will kill you," Nathan countered with good humor, causing Jake to smile in spite of the crappy circumstances.

"Yeah, believe it," Jaci piped in as she came into the room, carrying a carafe of coffee and mugs for them.

"I didn't survive all that crap with Nathan just to lose him now."

"It's going to be okay," Nathan promised her, but Jake shifted his gaze away, not wanting to lie to his future sister-in-law. Jaci was a good person, the perfect woman for Nathan and she was pretty tough, but he could see the worry in her stare.

They traded plans, going over every detail, every bit of minutiae important to the covert mission, and by the time Jake hit the couch for some shut-eye, he felt ready. Maybe it was suicidal, but he felt confident that he would prevail. Maybe he was delusional but he'd take it because it beat being scared spitless.

They would leave at first light, which made it imperative that he catch some sleep, but just as he was about to close his eyes, he heard Jaci come into the living room where he was crashing. He wasn't surprised when she kneeled down beside him in the darkness. "What's up?" he asked, rising on his elbow. "You okay?"

"No. I'm scared. I know how things can go bad in an instant. I don't want to lose you or Nathan. Nathan says not to worry but unlike you two, I'm not military trained. I'm a graphic designer who happened to fall in love with a man from a completely different world and if I hadn't been dragged into what happened a few months ago, I'd have no idea how to handle what's about to happen now. But even though I'm not that naive woman that I was, it's still hard to handle knowing that I could lose you both."

"I wish I could give you assurances that everything will be okay but I won't lie to you…things could go south. I can tell you that I'm going to try like hell to come out of this alive because I have no desire to die anytime soon and neither does Nathan."

She nodded but he could feel her worry as a tangible thing between them. "He wouldn't think of letting you do this on your own. No matter what you say."

"I know."

"He really loves you. I know he made some mistakes but he's trying to make amends."

"I know that, too." He sighed. "Listen, things are complicated between me and my brother but this time around he's been there for me and I appreciate his help. I really do, but my head is filled with all the crap that went down when he left me behind and it's hard to let that go."

"I just want you to know that it means a lot to him that he's there for you now because he couldn't be when you were kids. I don't know everything that happened—Nathan's told me a few things and it breaks my heart—but you can't live in the past forever, right? Especially when someone is trying to create a different future. So I want you to do your damnedest to come back in one piece so the love of my life doesn't have to go charging in after you. You both have to come back. You hear me? *Both of you.* You're my family now and I'm not about to let go without a fight."

Jake smiled at the fierceness in her tone. "Roger

that." He paused before saying, "I haven't had a sister for a long time. I imagine that if Bunny had lived, she would've been like you—strong, protective and woe be to anyone who stood between her and her brothers. My brother is a lucky man."

"And so is your scientist," Jaci countered warmly, giving his biceps a sisterly squeeze. "Sleep tight, Jakey."

Jaci padded silently from the room and Jake heard the bedroom door close softly. What would it be like to have the privilege of sleeping beside Kat each night? He craved her soft, delicate body curled against his. In a frighteningly short amount of time, he'd become addicted to Kat and everything that made her unique. He sent a silent prayer to any god that might be within earshot that Kat was safe. "I'm coming for you, babe," he promised under his breath. "I won't stop until you're safe or I'm dead."

Jake closed his eyes and forced himself to rest. He needed to be sharp tomorrow. So much was riding on his success.

Chapter 22

In a deserted building owned by the Defense Intelligence Department, Miles held court among the filthy rich individuals and countries who wanted MCX-209 for their own purposes.

"You said it would be ready by now," Mr. Blue reminded Miles tersely, shifting his gaze around the room, hating that he wasn't the only person with knowledge of the formula. "My buyer is running out of patience. Perhaps you oversold what you think you have."

There were grumbles of assent around the room and Miles held up his hand to quell the discontent. "Gentlemen, this is a highly sensitive process. We cannot rush something so groundbreaking or else we end up with something useless. My scientist is working around the clock, I assure you, to perfect the formula. We are close. The last round of test subjects showed promising results."

"Show us. We want to see it in action."

"Of course," Miles said. "And I have arranged the perfect show for you tonight."

That changed their tune. Suddenly, their expressions of ire morphed into keen excitement. "And where will this demonstration take place?"

"At an undisclosed location. Forgive me, but such precautions are necessary to safeguard some national secrets."

"You are willing to sell this drug beneath the nose of your country and yet you profess to want to protect government secrets?" Mr. Blue mocked. "You, Mr. Jogan, are a hypocrite."

A thin smile spread across Miles's lips. He hated Mr. Blue. "Perhaps. But old habits die hard, I suppose. Nevertheless, you will be escorted by car to the location, blindfolded, of course."

"I don't like this plan," another said, growling.

"That part is nonnegotiable. Either you go as directed or you don't go at all."

"How about I put a bullet in your head and take your scientist for myself. I can set up a lab just as easily as you."

"That is ill-advised, Mr. Kapoor. And if you threaten me again, my agent will put a bullet between your eyes." Miles flicked his stare to Camille who emerged from the shadows like a menacing spirit, gun trained on Mr. Kapoor, who startled when he realized how close he'd come to death. "Now, no more of this ugliness. We are standing on the precipice of a major breakthrough in neuroscience. Imagine the applications. The coordinates of the pickup have been relayed to your phone. Don't be late, gentlemen. It's going to be a fantastic show."

After the buyers had funneled out of the room and dispatched to their hotel rooms, Camille returned, a sour expression on her face. He frowned with irritation. He wasn't accustomed to Camille raining on his parade and he certainly didn't appreciate it now. "What's wrong?" he asked.

"Did you come on to that scientist woman?" Camille demanded in a show of female jealousy that was very unattractive. Miles showed his displeasure with the deepening of his frown but Camille wasn't deterred. "Well? That wasn't part of the plan. Perhaps you'd forgotten?"

"I've forgotten nothing. Where is this coming from?" he asked. "I have neither the time nor patience to field silly female insecurities."

"And I don't appreciate being played," Camille countered with deadly calm, all trace of female weakness gone. First and foremost Camille was a soldier and he didn't doubt that she wouldn't hesitate to kill him if betrayed. A flare of arousal followed the threat of danger. Damn his lust for risk. "I do not share," she reminded him.

"I am not asking you to share. I was merely trying to find a way to persuade Dr. Odgers to work willingly."

"What does it matter if she works willingly?" Camille asked, her lip sneering. "As long as she gets the work done, that's all that matters."

"A willing slave works harder than a captive one, my dear," he told her patiently, though his mind was working quickly. He'd always held the upper hand with Camille, but now he saw suspicion in her eyes that didn't bode well for either of them. If he couldn't trust her implicitly, she was of no use to him. He made a quick decision to lose her as soon as the deal was done and the money wired to his accounts. She was easily replaced in his bed and as his partner. Besides, he didn't like to share, either. He forced a warm smile and pulled her into his arms. "Darling, you're such a hothead. Come, let us put that passion to good use. We have a few hours to kill before we're needed again."

She softened against him and he knew she was once again his to command. Women, he sighed privately, were so high maintenance.

Kat stared at the formula, her vision swimming. What was she doing wrong? The answer felt so close but agonizingly far. The effect on victims—or test subjects as Camille called them—had ranged in destruction, with Anna being the least damaged, but that wasn't saying much. If she lived to be a hundred—which she knew she wouldn't—she would never forget Anna, the drug-addicted mom who'd just wanted to get better so she could go back to her kids.

The lab door slid open and Miles walked in, looking his usual debonair and wicked self, and it took everything in her not to sneer and say something reckless. She was operating on too little sleep and not enough real food and her self-preservation meter was running pretty low. "What do you want?" she asked sourly.

"I have news. Tonight we are scheduling a special presentation with the drug. How are the latest test subjects?"

She leaped from her stool. "I told you, it's not ready! The test subjects are ruined! As in totally brain dead. The only improvement so far has been that this time their brains didn't ooze from their ears! You're a monster for making me do this to people!"

"Settle down and quit the hysterics, please," he said. "We are close. I can feel it. But I think what's missing here is that added component of motivation. At first I thought you might be sufficiently motivated if your uncle were among the next test subjects but then I realized that would be a waste of a sample as his brain is already mush. Then, I realized, the most perfect candidate."

"And who would that be?" Kat was almost afraid to find out.

A smile formed on his lips and it was the most frightening sight she'd seen in days—and that included the brain ooze. "I want it to be a surprise. But I'll leave you with this… You'll want to be sure the formula works."

"I'm already trying as hard as I can! You think I enjoy watching these poor people suffer? You're a monster! I can't work any harder than I already am." Tears stung her eyes but she was too tired to hide them. "Please don't make me do this anymore. I'd rather die than administer this awful drug to anyone else."

"If death is what you seek, I can help you out—when the job is complete. Until then, get to work."

Miles left Kat sobbing with hopelessness and bewilderment. Who could he have that would make her work harder? She was already working her tush off with marginal results. She needed a break, to rest her brain so she could recharge but Miles gave her no opportunity to rest.

Focus, Kat. Stop crying. Someone else is going to die if you don't figure out what is going wrong. It took a moment but slowly her sobs turned to painful hiccups and she was able to wash her face with cold water.

Maybe she was going about it all wrong. She was trying to perfect the drug so that it reacted in the same way, each time with permanent results. What if she could make the results temporary? Just long enough to fool Miles but would slowly dissipate with time? The subtle change in direction sparked her frazzled brain, giving it the much-needed boost of power.

She already knew Miles planned to kill her when the work was finished. If she were able to make the drug temporary without Miles's knowledge, then he would end up killing her without realizing that his drug was useless. Ultimately, his buyers would be outraged that they'd been duped and Miles would spend the rest of his life looking over his shoulder rather than lounging on a beach somewhere drinking a fruity beverage. That sounded good to Kat. She'd prefer Miles go to prison but if that wasn't going to happen, she'd settle for misery.

Armed with a newfound sense of purpose, Kat began deconstructing the formula to start from scratch. The answer was there—she just needed to find it.

Jake entered The Bunker, his expression carefully neutral as Miles approached. He was armed to the teeth with everything he'd need to accomplish his covert mission and he was in his element, though he never imagined he'd be using his skills to break into his own department's facility.

Miles shook his hand vigorously as if he were truly relieved to see Jake had escaped the hit, and patted him on the back a few times. "Good to see you, son. You can't believe how happy I am that you were smart enough to thwart whoever is trying to take you down. I want you to know that I've launched a full-scale investigation into finding the mole but in the meantime I want you to lay low."

"Sounds good to me," Jake agreed. "Have you managed to relocate Dr. Odgers? I was a little concerned when you sent Camille to take over. Any reason for that? I confess, I felt that perhaps you blamed me for the people coming after us. Now that you know there is a mole, I'm in the clear, right?"

"Yes, yes, absolutely. And I don't want you to worry about Dr. Odgers. She is in safe hands. In fact, if you like I will arrange a meeting so you can rest assured that she is fine."

"Would you mind? That would be great. I feel responsible for her, seeing as my mission was compromised. Feels like a loose end."

"Of course. You're a good agent. That's only natural. How about in an hour?"

"Is she here? In The Bunker?" he asked, feigning surprise.

"For the time being. We're still arranging her new identity. Takes time, you know, to sew up those details."

Jake nodded as if he understood. "I'd appreciate the meeting, for closure."

"Then you shall have your closure." Miles smiled and it took every ounce of strength not to grab him by the neck and shake the truth out of him. Jake returned the smile. "Okay, your room is L304. Do you remember how to get there?"

"Yes."

"Excellent. Let's meet again at 1800 hours in Lab 3."

Lab 3. That's probably where Miles was keeping Kat. Jake nodded. "Affirmative."

Miles grinned and they parted ways. Jake knew he was being watched, so he quickly headed in the direction of his room, just as he was expected to. But the minute he got to his room, he went into the bathroom, the one place where there wasn't surveillance, and peeled away the first fake skin patch on his inner thigh. He winced as it tore away hair in the process. Pressed inside the fake skin was a paper-thin film, which was encoded with prerecorded video feed. Timing it perfectly, he slid the film over the surveillance camera lens, where it immediately sucked to the glass. The minute it made contact, a prerecorded feed began to play, showing a resting Jake.

Then, he peeled the second fake skin patch from his forearm and went to the door panel where a thumbprint was needed for access. The technology was highly advanced but also wired into the Zephyr system. James had created a virus that could be picked up by the thumbprint scan.

"Please work," he whispered as he carefully placed the film on the scanner where the thumb went. The scan did its job and for two heartbeats, nothing happened and Jake's hopes began to plummet but then, systematically, everything began to shut down.

"Yes! I owe you a beer, James Cotton," he said, leaving the room and hustling to Lab 3. He had five minutes to make this work or else all was lost. Running down the halls, he found Lab 3 and quickly entered, searching wildly for Kat.

"Kat!" he called out, navigating the darkness, bang-ing his knee on something. "Damn it, Kat…are you in here?"

"Jake?" a tremulous voice answered, and he nearly stumbled with relief. "Is that you?"

"Yes! I've come to rescue you. Come on, we don't have much time." He found her hand and gave it a squeeze for reassurance. Her skin felt cold and clammy and he wondered if Miles had kept her holed up in this lab the entire time. Likely so. He gentled his voice, but kept the urgency. "We have to get out of here. We only have a window of five minutes before the system kicks back on."

"There's no way out of this place," she whispered fearfully. "It's hell." She stopped suddenly. "Wait…they told me you were dead. Are you dead? Oh, my God, am I dead? Maybe I died from exhaustion? Maybe I'm hallucinating? I don't know what's real anymore."

She was cracking up. Jake stopped and pulled her to him, clutching her tightly. "Neither you nor I are dead but we will be if we don't get the hell out of here, pronto."

"Jake? It's really you?" The tremulous hope in her voice cut him in two and he knew they didn't have time for this but he couldn't stop himself. A desperate hunger to taste her again took over and he slanted his mouth over hers, and a near delirium followed as pure joy cascaded through him. Kat was in his arms again. Kat was everything he never knew he needed and he'd sacrifice his life to know she was safe.

She sagged in his arms, whimpering, and moisture dribbled down to their lips, which told him she was crying. "Shh," he whispered. "It's going to be okay. I promise."

She nodded with a slight hiccup and he clutched her hand in his, drawing her toward the exit. They'd lost precious time but if they hustled they could make it out of there.

Sickly green emergency lights glowed along the seam of the floor, lending a creepy color to the walls as they ran. Blaring sirens sounded as people rushed past them, oblivious to Kat and Jake. Jake rounded the final corner, daring to hope that they'd actually made it when the lights flipped on and Jake found himself face-to-face with Miles Jogan and a cadre of armed guards. Kat screamed and stumbled back as Jake placed himself between her and the guards.

"Something tells me you've been less than honest, Agent Isaacs," Miles said, gesturing to the guards who approached them both, heavily armed. "Take them to Lab 2, if you would. We don't want to be late for the presentation."

Kat paled and started to shake her head. "Please! No...!" She began to kick and scream as a guard wrenched her away from Jake just as another guard put him in handcuffs. She looked wildly to Miles, pleading. "Please...not Jake. Don't do this. I beg you!"

"Begging does not become you, Dr. Odgers. I told

you I believed you lacked sufficient motivation. I believe Agent Isaacs will definitely help motivate you."

"Nooooo!"

The guards dragged Kat away and her screams echoed down the hallway. Jake turned a hard glare Miles's way. There was little point in pretending now. "What are you going to do with me?"

"You are going to be my star attraction as Dr. Odgers proves that her drug works. Think of this as a blessing… with your memory gone I'll have no need to kill you. Contrary to what you may believe, I always liked you. You reminded me of myself in a different life. But business is business and you're going to help fund my future."

"What's going to happen to Kat?" he asked, already knowing the answer.

"What does it matter? In a matter of minutes you won't even remember her."

"You bastard!"

"I've been called worse." Miles gestured to the guards. "Lab 2, please."

And then Jake was marched in the same direction as Kat to a fate worse than death.

Chapter 23

Tears streaming down her numb cheeks, Kat stared in horror as Miles's guards muscled Jake into a sitting position and clamped their hands on his shoulders to keep him there. Jake met her gaze and tried to reassure her but she knew their odds were bad. Worse, she hadn't been able to test the new sample with her modifications. She had no idea if it worked or would cause Jake's brain to explode like an egg thrown at a wall. She couldn't bear the idea of being the one who killed Jake. The pressure was too much and the stakes too high. "I—I can't do this," she stammered, her hands shaking when she tried to lift the syringe. Miles took his gun and pointed it at Jake's head.

"Either inject him or I shoot him. Your choice."

"He could die either way," she whispered in total misery. "That's not a fair choice."

"Life is not fair. With a bullet, death is a certainty. If you've done your job and corrected the formula, he will live. The power is in your hands, Dr. Odgers."

"Please! Please! I can't do this! I can't!"

"Dr. Odgers, you're embarrassing yourself. Inject the formula or watch him die!"

She looked to Jake, her eyesight swimming with desperate tears and she wanted to die herself rather than plunge that needle in Jake's arm.

"It's okay," Jake said softly, trying to calm her, which was so endearing and yet so ridiculous.

"You don't understand. It could kill you in the most horrifying way," she explained to Jake, her throat closing as fear and misery crawled up her esophagus and her bladder suddenly ached. "Th-the test subjects… some died with their brains leaking out of their ears. I can't take that risk of it happening to you. I'd rather die myself."

Motivated by sheer hopelessness, Kat grabbed the syringe and went to plunge it into her own arm but quicker than she would've imagined, Miles caught her just before the needle pierced her skin and pried the syringe free, crushing her fingers in the process. She cried out as he pushed her away in disgust. "That was ill-advised, Doctor," he said as she crashed against her lab stool and nearly fell over. "Agent Stephens, please restrain the good doctor for her own protection."

"Certainly, sir," Camille said, jerking Kat to her feet and pinioning her arms behind her back.

"I'm sorry, Jake," she whispered, unable to tear her eyes away from the man she was certain was her soul mate and possibly about to die because of her.

"Shut it," Camille warned, pinching her arms together more tightly until Kat gasped with the pain. "You don't want to miss the show."

A million obscenities danced on her tongue but she held them back. *Please, please let the modifications work.* She closed her eyes and took a few deep breaths. When she opened her eyes again, she at least didn't want to retch as she trained her gaze forward.

Miles smiled with approval. "That a girl. A professional. I like that in a person." He looked to the guards. "Bring in our guests."

The guards opened the doors and a group of eight men filed in. Kat gave them each a hard stare, letting them know exactly how she felt about them. They were all evil wretches and she hoped that karma rained down on them with a vengeance.

"Gentlemen, we have a real treat for you tonight. The subject is a perfect specimen. Smart, fit and top of his graduating class in officer school."

Murmurs of interest sounded in the room and Kat wanted to scream. Jake glared at the men as if mentally cataloging their faces for when he escaped. She loved him for his indomitable spirit, but she knew their chances of rescue or escape were slim to none at this point. She savored the memory of their last kiss, even though it might've been what cost them precious time.

"What admittedly started out as a drug for Alzheimer's patients has turned into a boon for people such as you with specific needs. I give you MCX-209, or as I like to call it, The Game Changer."

A ripple of amused laughter followed and Kat seethed at their heartless cruelty. She sent Miles her most hateful stare. She hoped he died in a horrible accident that left him to linger until he finally breathed his last breath. She'd always fancied herself a bit of a liberal and against the death penalty but at this moment she would've paid to flip the switch herself on Miles Jogan and his cohort, Camille Stephens.

"Enough with the small talk, let's start the show," Miles announced to polite applause. "Dr. Odgers, if you would do the honors of administering your amazing drug."

Camille whispered in her ear, "If you pull another stunt like you just did, I'll drag your loony uncle from his bed and shoot him so full of holes, he'll leak like a sieve. Got it?"

"You're a hateful human being," Kat whispered back, but jerked away from Camille and straightened her lab coat to collect herself. She lifted her gaze to Jake and knew she had no choice but to give him the drug. He knew it, too, and nodded faintly as if to tell her he understood and didn't blame her.

It was that gentle sweetness that nearly caused her

knees to buckle as she approached Jake with the syringe. She wanted to beg Jake's forgiveness for doing this to him but in his eyes there was no judgment, if anything, all she saw was love. *Love?* Kat blinked, sure she was hallucinating. But no. Jake's gaze softened in the face of her turmoil and she nearly crumpled to the ground in the wake of such grace.

"I'm sorry," she whispered, gently taking his wrist and plunging the needle as painlessly as possible. She mouthed the words she read in his expression and he closed his eyes with an imperceptible nod. Kat used to think that the story of Romeo and Juliet was so romantic but now she realized it wasn't romantic at all—it was a tragedy.

She held her breath. The new modification to the formula was supposed to react much more quickly than before. If the changes were going to work, they'd see the effects almost immediately. Kat chewed on her bottom lip, terrified. Miles started explaining the process to his guests.

"What's happening here is the drug is working its way through the bloodstream, where it will take an express elevator to the neurological center of the brain. Once there, it will start working on the area tasked with memory. Dr. Odgers has been working diligently to perfect the formula and—" he stopped to peer at Jake "—seeing as he hasn't begun to convulse, I take that as a sign that her hard work has paid off."

More polite laughter until suddenly Jake jerked and

spasmed painfully, causing Kat to stuff her knuckle in her mouth to keep from screaming as she watched in total terror as Jake began to shake uncontrollably. Miles chuckled a bit nervously as he added, "Maybe I spoke too soon…"

But as suddenly as the spasms started, they ended, and Jake slumped in his chair, listless and still but alive.

Miles turned to his assembled guests with a lifted brow, acting like the ringleader in a three-ringed circus. "I believe we have success…Agent Isaacs…where were you born?" For a long moment Jake said nothing. He stared into space as if Miles hadn't spoken.

Kat began to quake as the fear that she'd permanently ruined Jake's amazing brain took hold. But it was a good sign that he hadn't begun to leak from the ears, so she took hope in that, however small.

"Agent Isaacs…where were you born?"

"I…I don't know," he answered in a slow, tortured voice. His fine motor skills seemed dampened as he swung his head toward Miles without an ounce of recognition and Kat swallowed a cry of both relief and horror. The drug had worked. But she had no idea what the side effects would be or if Jake would ever be able to recover his memories. "Where…am…I?"

"You're in a safe place," Miles assured Jake in a soft voice, then turned to his guests with a triumphant, smug smile. "I give you…The Game Changer."

"How do we know he's not faking it?" a small Indian man demanded, not quite convinced.

"Dr. Odgers, will you provide a brain scan of Agent Isaacs for our guests?"

Kat jerked a nod and the guards pulled Jake from his chair roughly. "Be easy with him," she cried, shooting a look at Miles for his guards' lack of concern. She hissed at the guards, "How would you like your brain erased? I have plenty left in my samples."

The guards shifted with discomfort at her threat but Miles found her amusing, saying, "That, my friends, is a feisty woman. Glad she's working for us."

She shot him a look that said, *Screw you, Miles,* and took a quick scan of Jake's brain, not only for Miles but for herself. She needed to see the extent of the damage. The areas of the brain holding memory were indeed affected as intended, and Kat had to hold back tears. "The brain has two areas designated for memory—one for long-term and another for short-term. The subject—" she swallowed the lump in her throat at referring to Jake as a test subject "—exhibits the appropriate signs that both long-term and short-term memory have been erased but none of the autonomic nervous systems have been affected."

"So he won't forget how to stop breathing or swallow?" one person asked.

"No."

"Excellent," he murmured, impressed. "This is indeed a game changer."

"What did I tell you? Gentlemen, the bidding will begin in fifteen minutes. Reserve is set at ten million."

Miles shepherded the men from the room and paused to say to the guards, "See to it that Dr. Odgers and Agent Isaacs are given some rest. They've had a busy day."

To Kat he said, "Brilliant work, Dr. Odgers. You have my utmost respect for your talent."

"I don't want your respect. I want your head on a platter," she retorted dully, not caring about self-preservation at this point.

"So feisty…" he murmured, and let himself out.

The guards led Kat and Jake from the lab and dumped them both in her tiny room. She allowed her surprise to show and the guard on the left gave her a subtle nod, so subtle she almost thought she imagined it. But what did it matter? Their lives were on the short track. Miles had no reason to keep them alive.

She went to Jake and grasped his hand. He looked to her with a wide, almost blank stare and asked with difficulty, "Do…I…know…you?"

She nodded and wiped her tears away. "I'm sorry," she whispered. "This is all my fault. I'm so sorry."

"Don't…cry."

A tiny, almost hysterical bubble of laughter followed as she kissed his hand. Bossy even with a brain blowout. "I love you, Jake Isaacs. God, I love you."

Jake stared past Kat, bewildered, probably wondering why he couldn't remember anything. She couldn't imagine anything more startling than to discover that your memories were a blank slate. Kat started talking, maybe to ease the silence or maybe to avoid facing the horrible reality. "When my uncle first showed signs of Alzheimer's, the signs were very small. Little things he'd forget, names and places, mostly, but then as things got worse, he started to forget where he lived and he would wander. It got so that he couldn't be trusted to be alone. I had to hire a babysitter for him but then he wouldn't listen to the babysitter, either. It was exhausting chasing after him. I felt guilty for putting him in that facility but relieved, too. But I told myself if I could manufacture a cure, then I could make it better for him." Kat stopped as her throat closed. She inhaled a sharp breath and forced herself to continue. "I was so close. I pushed forward when I knew I should've stopped. But it was so tantalizing, the idea that I might create a cure for Alzheimer's. My ego put us here. I'm no better than Miles Jogan," she finished with an agonized whisper.

Kat didn't know the extent of the damage to Jake's brain, nor what kind of damage would be permanent. She didn't know what to think of his sluggish mental faculties but could only hope that part would fade eventually. But what did she know? Maybe it was irreversible. God, she hoped not. She wanted Jake to argue with her, call her stubborn or comment on her quirky personality. She wanted him to give her that special look that gave her shivers. Would she ever get her Jake back?

Maybe it was all a moot point. Miles wouldn't suffer them to live for too long. Kat slipped her hand into

Jake's and leaned against him, closing her eyes for a moment because she was literally exhausted.

Kat had only closed her eyes for a moment when she heard gunshots. Startling, she wondered what was going on. A part of her leaped with hope at the idea that someone was storming this underground prison looking for them but the odds of that were very low. With any luck, Miles Jogan took a bullet to the balls in the skirmish.

Suddenly, the door opened and Kat jumped back, terrified that she was about to meet her maker, but two men she didn't recognize rushed in and one went straight to Jake while the other stood at the door with his gun ready.

"No…no…Jakey?" The man grabbed Jake's chin and stared hard into his eyes but there was zero recognition in them. "What happened to him?" he demanded, nearly yelling at Kat.

"H-he's been given MCX-209. His memory is gone," she stammered an answer, looking at the man, who seemed a bigger, rawer version of Jake. "Who are you?"

"I'm his brother. Come on, we're getting the hell out of here. You must be Kat?" he guessed as he shouldered Jake. At her nod, he said, "We have to get him to the hospital. Follow me."

"How'd you get in?" she asked, hurrying after the man. "What's your name?"

"My name is Nathan and we got in with a little help from a virus and my friend, Holden. Michelle Rainier, Jake's top superior, caught wind of Miles Jogan's extracurricular activity and decided to check in herself. While we were able to access the facility, Rainier assembled her own team and found Jogan operating his little freak show. Tell me what we can do for Jake."

Holden paused to take a quick look at Jake and the only change in his expression was the minute twitch in his eyebrow as he said to Kat, "He looks brain dead. Your drug did this?"

Kat nodded with misery. "I didn't want to. Miles made me. Trust me, I wish I'd never created it."

Holden grunted with a nod then jerked his head at Nathan, as if to say, *let's blow this joint,* and Kat was happy to obey.

"It's not your fault. No one blames you," Nathan said quickly, adjusting his brother as they hurried down the hallway. "Is there anything we can do to help him?"

"I don't know," she admitted, scared to death that Nathan would eventually hate her when he realized Jake may never be the same. "I made modifications to the formula in the hopes of making the drug's effects temporary but I hadn't had the chance to test the new formula before Miles made me inject Jake."

"That bastard is going to pay," Nathan growled. "He'd better hope my brother recovers."

Kat nodded, anguish caught in her chest at the reality facing Jake's recovery. Nathan didn't blame her at the moment because they had bigger problems and that's probably what Nathan was focusing on but eventually, when Jake's recovery slowed to a crawl—if he recovered at all—Nathan might change his tune. She swallowed the fear and forced herself to focus on the here and now. A miracle would be greatly appreciated, she thought with a quick prayer.

They passed Miles as a very stern-looking woman was handcuffing him. Kat knew she ought to keep going but there was no way she was going to pass up the opportunity to give Miles what he deserved, if even in the smallest measure. Before Nathan could stop her, she walked right up to Miles and slapped him as hard as she could right across the mouth. The impact stung her hand but it felt good. "I hope they stick you someplace dark and dank and you never see the sunlight ever again," she spat. "A prison cell is too good for you."

The woman paused, lifting a penciled brow at Kat's sudden act of violence. "And you are?" she asked, her gaze flicking to Nathan, Jake and Holden, but her attention seemed focused on Kat.

"I'm Dr. Kat Odgers. I created MCX-209."

"If you were smart you'd keep this woman under lock and key," Miles said, glaring at Kat, still attempting to exert some authority even though he had none. "She's got the power to create the world's biggest weapon. If not me, then someone else is going to find her and finish what I started."

The woman ignored Miles but Kat could feel the tension growing between Nathan and Holden, who clearly wanted to do some damage to Miles, as well.

For a long moment, the woman regarded Kat with

interest but then her gaze flicked to Miles and she said, "We'll be in touch. The guards tell me your uncle is also in this facility?" she asked, and Kat nodded. "We'll return him to his managed care facility." To Nathan she said, "Take him home. A hospital can do nothing for him. Isn't that right, Dr. Odgers?"

She nodded, a little in awe of this powerful woman that Kat had to assume was Michelle Rainier.

"Take him home so he can rest. If he's going to recover, it will happen surrounded by things he knows."

Kat wasn't sure about that but it was a worth a try. Honestly, she'd happily go anywhere as long as it was away from this underground hell. "Thank you," she said with tears in her eyes.

"Don't thank me yet. We still have to work out what's going to happen with that drug of yours. I think you know we can't let that out into the world…in anyone's hands."

Kat knew that all too well. She'd do whatever she needed to make things right.

Chapter 24

Jake knew that a terrible drug had affected his memory. He knew that the man who gave him anxious looks was his brother and he knew he used to work for a U.S. government department called the Defense Intelligence, but he only knew these things because that's what he'd been told. He had no recollection of these facts and it freaked him out.

On a certain level, it felt as if people were making up his personal history because there was absolutely no connection on his part to any of the things he'd been told. The guy identified as his brother, Nathan, looked ready to beat someone to a pulp over what'd been done to him. According to the woman who'd been forced to give him the drug, Kat, the drug was supposed to wear off but it'd been a few days with only subtle improvements and he'd given up hope that anything would change.

"How are you feeling today?" Kat asked, coming into the room where Jake was staring out the front window, watching people and cars go by on the residential street. Jake turned and shrugged. "About the same?"

"Yeah," he answered. He knew she felt personally responsible for what had happened to him but from the events that had been told to him, it wasn't her fault. She was as much a victim as anyone else.

"I think I must've miscalculated something—again. The effects should've worn off by now," she said, worrying her lip and appearing ready to burst into tears.

He may not remember her but when he looked at her, something like sunshine on a warm day spread throughout his chest. He didn't know why but he liked it.

"I'm so sorry, Jake. I don't know what to do to fix this."

"Maybe with more time," he suggested, though he didn't hold out hope. Her soft brown hair was pulled back from her face and he caught a good look at her eyes—a striking green that shone like polished jade— and he wondered if she knew how beautiful she was. He wished he could remember more about their history. Thus far, Kat had been unwilling to talk much about it, saying she didn't want to unduly influence his memory. But the way he saw it, maybe talking about it was the key. "Was I in love with you?" he asked, startling her with his soft query. "Because when I look at you, I feel something different than when I look at the rest of the people around me."

"I—I don't know…maybe…I mean, yes, I think you were," she admitted, tears starting to collect in her eyes. "But we'd only known each other a short time so maybe it was just the extreme situation we were in."

"Maybe," he said, but as soon as she suggested it, his chest tightened and he knew that wasn't the case. He'd felt something real with this woman and he wanted it back. An idea struck him. He'd been watching copious amounts of television to catch up on current events and in the midst of zoning out on CNN, a commercial for improving memory had flashed across the screen. He wondered if something like that might help him. "You say my brain isn't exactly physically damaged…maybe we can retrain my brain to remember things?"

"Like how?"

"I don't know. Brain games? I saw this commercial on CNN, after watching an entire segment about the current struggle in Afghanistan," he said.

Kat considered his suggestion, frowning slightly as she processed—a little habit he noticed she did often and he found really cute. "Maybe…we could try it," she said. "Let me do some research and I'll get back to you about it."

He nodded, then reached up to gently pull her hair free from its elastic. "There…that's better." He slid his fingers through the strands. "Your hair is so soft." He leaned forward and inhaled deeply, surprised by the jolt he felt when the familiar scent hit his olfactory senses. Something about that scent… "I remember something," he said with growing excitement. "Something about you…"

"Of course!" Kat exclaimed as if she should've known. "The olfactory sense is the closest shortcut to memory the brain has! Come, smell my neck. You used to nuzzle my neck—it was your favorite spot, you said."

Jake didn't hesitate and pulled her into his arms. This felt right. He buried his nose against the soft flesh of her neck and inhaled deeply. The scent of warm female skin tingled in his nostril and he closed his eyes as a flash of something raced across his mind. He tightened his hold on Kat, and she released a tiny moan as if she couldn't help herself. He pressed an exploratory kiss on the pliant skin, his lips nibbling as he went, and while it felt like heaven to hold her like this, nothing more than that momentary sizzle erupted in his memory. He sighed, knowing it had been too much to hope for.

She stilled in his arms and she knew that they'd been denied their miracle. She tried to pull away but he didn't want to let her go. "I don't remember you," he admitted. "But I remember the way I *feel* when I'm around you. There's something inside my heart that remembers you even if my brain doesn't."

She nodded but when he finally let her go, tears sparkled in her eyes. "I don't think I can live with what I've done, not only to you but to the others," she said in a tortured voice. "There were so many others in that place who suffered far more than you—who died horrible deaths—because of this drug. I see their faces when I sleep at night and I don't know how much more I can handle."

"It wasn't your fault."

"It doesn't matter. I still carry the guilt. I should've been strong enough to kill myself before Miles could make me give those innocent people that injection but I was too much of a coward."

"Stop that. Don't talk about dying," he said roughly. Just the thought of Kat not being around filled him with panic. "We'll get this figured out."

She cupped his face, her expression sad. "Jake…the drug should've worn off by now. These effects might be permanent. I don't think I can bear the thought that I did this to you. It's killing me inside."

"So we make new memories," he said stubbornly. "You're the only one who makes me feel anything. That has to mean something. I think if we give it more time, the drug will wear off because even though I don't have my memory back I have improved. I could barely speak a few days ago," he reminded her. She nodded but the sadness radiating from her nearly broke his heart. This time, he cupped her face. "Please don't give up on me."

"I could never give up on you but, for the safety of the world, the knowledge of MCX-209 needs to go away. I think I should take the injection, too."

"No!" he said emphatically. "Don't even think about doing something so reckless. I won't let you."

"Jake, there's still the threat hanging over our heads. Someone is going to find out that I made that damn drug and I'll always have to look over my shoulder. I don't want to live that way. Your boss Michelle Rainier has arranged for me to have a new identity but if someone really wants to find out who I am, they'll do it and this nightmare will start all over again. I never want to put my loved ones at risk again."

"I understand and maybe it's selfish of me to beg you not to do it, but I feel as if everything that made me, me, the essence of who I truly am, is housed safely in your head. If that goes away…I truly won't have existed at all. And there's something else…I don't want you to stop looking at me the way you do," he admitted, drawing her close to sweep a kiss across her lips. She sagged against him as a sob fell from her lips. He kissed her harder, needing to feel her against him, and as she responded, clinging to him as tightly as he clung to her, something inside his brain shifted and another dizzying volley of emotion nearly tumbled him to the ground. "You're the key to my recovery," he whispered against her mouth. "Please stick with me. We're so close. Promise you won't give up on me."

"I promise," she choked out the words. "I promise."

Jake held her as she cried and a few tears of his own leaked from his eyes but he knew he could come back from this if Kat helped him. It was his gut instinct that told him to not let her go and while he didn't remember his previous life with the DID, somehow he sensed that that gut instinct had kept him alive on many occasions, so he was going to pay sharp attention to whatever little signals came his way.

Later that night as he stared up at the night sky, Nathan joined him. They sat in silence for a long moment until his brother started talking, as if to fill the void between them.

"I haven't told you everything about our relationship," Nathan started, his voice heavy with something painful. "Before you got injected with that drug, you were harboring some serious anger against me and it was warranted."

Jake didn't know what to think of that. He didn't know this man, and thus felt no animosity toward him. "Don't feel compelled to confess your sins or apologize for crimes I don't remember," he said. "I don't know what beef I had with you but you seem a pretty decent guy now, so let's just let it go at that."

"I wish I could. But I have to get something off my chest. Once I've said my piece, you can do with it what you want. Okay?"

"I guess. If you feel you have to."

Nathan nodded and pushed forward with an air of determination as if he needed courage to continue. "Our childhood was shit. Our parents were no-good abusive losers who didn't deserve a fish much less three kids."

"Three?"

"We had a sister, Bunny. She died when she was six."

Somehow the pain of not remembering a sister who had died hurt more than anything. "What was she like?" he asked.

Nathan paused to pull the memory free. Jake imagined it was as painful for Nathan to remember as it was for him to realize he'd forgotten. "She was always smiling, no matter what—even when she was doing something she shouldn't. She had an impish spirit and loved to play hide-and-seek."

"What happened to her?"

"Our mother backed over her with the station wagon we owned. I was supposed to be watching her, but I was arguing with you about something stupid and took my eyes off her for a minute. The next thing I knew, everyone was screaming and Bunny was dead."

Jake stared at his brother, unable to fathom the guilt he must carry. It was too much for one person to carry alone. "You were a kid, hardly old enough to be watching over two siblings without supervision," Jake said, trying to ease the pain he saw in Nathan's eyes. "You have to let that go."

Nathan nodded as if he knew that logically but rational thought never shared a bed with the emotional heart. "I tell myself that but it's hard, especially when your parents blame you for what happened, too. I think Bunny was the only kid they actually cared about."

"I'm beginning to think that forgetting certain memories is a blessing," Jake admitted.

"Yeah, I wouldn't mind losing a few," Nathan agreed. "We had the worst parents I can ever imagine. And we only had each other. But I couldn't take another minute of living in that house and I split the first chance I got, leaving you behind in the process. I made you a promise that night to come back and get you but I joined the marines and didn't see you again until recently. I wanted to come back, but circumstances were never right and by the time I had the resources, you were already in the army, making your own mark on the world and I figured I was the last person you wanted to see, anyway. And I was right. What I'm trying to say is, you had every reason to hate me and I wouldn't feel right not admitting that to you and pretending like it never happened just because you can't remember."

Jake didn't know what to say. He didn't feel any anger toward Nathan. Whatever had been there previously, had all been wiped away. "Sounds like you were a kid trying to survive. Nothing to apologize for, as far as I can tell. I can't say what I was feeling before I was injected with that drug but I do know that you pulled me from that bunker and you're helping me now, so whatever happened in the past…I'm thinking it can stay there."

And then tears sparkled in Nathan's eyes and Jake knew he'd said the right thing. It felt right, besides. Silence returned between them but this time, it no longer felt awkward, but simply comfortable. If he and Nathan had once been close, perhaps they could be again with time. Jake was open to that and grateful for a brother who wanted to rebuild something that had been broken so long ago.

Nathan left Jake on the porch and returned to the house where he found Holden nursing a beer, lost in his own thoughts. He'd managed to talk Holden into staying the night and he was glad because his friend wasn't looking so good. Not that he blamed him, the guy had lost his twin brother a few months ago and they'd been pretty close.

Nathan took a seat across from him and cracked his own beer, thankful to be in his own home and not that bunker. "You okay?" he asked Holden. "Thinking of Miko?"

Holden didn't answer right away. Then, he said, "I was thinking of that drug and how it's affected Jake. A part of me wished that Miko had taken the drug. Maybe he'd still be around if he hadn't been dogged by all that guilt."

"That's a slippery slope, man. That drug does more than just erase the painful memories—it takes all the good ones, too. Miko wouldn't have wanted that."

Holden nodded but the motion lacked conviction. Nathan sighed, knowing that as much as he missed his friend, Holden was missing his brother more. "I appreciate your help in this situation. I know it couldn't have been easy so soon after Miko's death."

"The world doesn't stop turning, right?" Holden finished his beer. "I know that but at times, I can't stop thinking about what happened and why."

"That's a first-class ticket to crazy. There's no unraveling what happened with Miko. Bad choices and even worse consequences. That's it. He was a good guy. Just remember that. That's what I do. He was my friend and that's how he'll remain in my memory. He was your brother and nothing will change that, either, no matter what the reports say about his conduct"

"Yeah, I know. But that's the thing…I think the reports are wrong."

Nathan stopped and stared at Holden. "What do you mean?"

"I've been doing some digging…I know ID has been shut down and that's all good, but I think there's more to the story. My brother wasn't the kind of guy who would do the things they said he did."

Nathan's spirits fell. He understood Holden's reluctance to believe what his brother had done but Nathan knew the facts, even if they were painful to accept. However, he also knew Holden didn't want to hear Nathan's opinion on it right now. "If you believe there's more to the story…don't give up until you're satisfied. That's what I would do."

Nathan knew that eventually Holden would have to come to the realization that Miko had indeed, simply taken a wrong turn, but until then, he wouldn't lose a friend by insisting on it.

"I'm real sorry about Jake," Holden said. "I hope he pulls through. Losing a brother…it's rough."

Nathan nodded, thankful that his brother was still alive and kicking, even if he was a bit dotty in the memory department.

"I'd give anything to have my brother back." Holden crushed his can and tossed it into the garbage before heading for the second guest bedroom and disappearing behind the closed door.

Nathan spent several minutes just sitting there, thinking of Miko and everything that had happened with Tessara and ID. He knew where Holden was coming from, hell, he'd lived through it and he didn't want to believe how badly things had gone down but did he believe that there was more to the picture than what they already knew? Not really. He hoped for Holden's sake that he found closure. Nathan was tired of all the subterfuge, secrets and lies. Too many lives had been messed with and he was done with it all.

Several weeks went by, filled with tense meetings with the Defense Intelligence Department, as Michelle Rainier tried to convince Kat to take on a new identity and leave Jake behind until Kat finally put her foot down and declared that she wasn't going anywhere without Jake and that was final.

"You can understand our concern with you remaining in the private sector," Michelle said. "That drug can never hit the streets."

"I won't leave Jake," Kat said, crossing her arms. "We love each other."

"How is his memory?" she asked.

"Improving every day. It takes work but he's beginning to remember small details."

Michelle nodded with approval at the promising news. "In your clinical opinion, do you feel a full recovery is possible?"

"With time," Kat answered carefully. "But if I had access to my lab notes I might be able to expedite the process."

"We've had our team of scientists studying your notes and I have to say that you're brilliant—and light-years ahead of anything we can replicate. I do wish your notes hadn't been coded, though. It's taken just as much time to decode your notes as it has to follow them."

"I'd say that's a good thing," Kat said. "I don't want anyone replicating what I've done."

Michelle leaned forward. "Come work for us."

Kat stared. Had this woman lost her mind? Work for the people who had caused all this turmoil? *Not a chance.*

Michelle saw the storm brewing in Kat's expression and said, "Hear me out. You're right in that even if we change your identity, nothing is foolproof. Someone might find out who you are and what you're capable of. However, if you work for us, we can grant you top security clearance with a sizable increase in income, which will enable you to continue working in your field, with better resources and top-notch security."

"People still might find out about MCX-209," Kat maintained stubbornly, not willing to take the chance. "It's too risky."

"We have resources. We can destroy all mention of the drug and its formula. Tessara Pharm has already relinquished all your data and scrubbed your computer of all notes pertaining to MCX-209. The only reference is here in this lab, which you could control if you were the department head."

To be department head of a state-of-the-art lab? The temptation pulled at the scientist in her but her heart was still leery. "What kind of work would I be doing here?" she asked, cautious curious. "Nothing illegal?"

"Nothing illegal. We follow strict guidelines set forth by the FDA in our drug trials. Our experiments are more cerebral than chemical. We employ the nation's top minds and I think you would fit in perfectly among our team of geniuses."

In another time, this offer would've been a dream come true. "What about Jake?" she asked.

"Jake is still a valuable member of this team. When he recovers, his job is waiting for him."

Kat chewed her lip in thought. Jake had expressed a concern about his future, what he was qualified to do, how he would provide a living now that his circumstances had changed—man stuff. A small smile followed at the private thought. Michelle was offering a chance to rebuild their lives—to move out of Nathan and Jaci's home—and start fresh. "Who would I answer to?" she asked.

"Me."

"And only you?"

"And only me."

Kat liked Michelle. She seemed a straight shooter and after Kat's ordeal, she appreciated that quality in a person. She had loved her lab, even if she'd been ordered to do evil things in it. Could she walk back into that lab and forget all the terrible things that happened there? No. But she suspected if she agreed to sign on the dotted line, Michelle could make some adjustments. "If I agreed, you'd have to meet some requests," Kat warned.

"Name them."

"I can't work in that lab again. It's tainted with what happened. I'll need a whole new lab."

Michelle laughed. "Understandable and that's easily met. You wouldn't be working in The Bunker—I'm in the process of decommissioning that facility. After what happened with Miles Jogan, I think it's best to distance ourselves from that place. My dear, you would be coming to Washington to work in a state-of-the-art lab there, not in some underground box in New Mexico."

"Oh!" Kat exclaimed, happier than she realized she'd be. "That makes a big difference in how I feel about your offer."

"Glad to hear it."

"One more thing… The people who died in that

place…I wanted to honor them in some way. They died needlessly."

"What did you have in mind? We have to tread cautiously. As far as the record is concerned, what happened in The Bunker never happened, as I'm sure you can understand."

"I know. But some of those people had families who might be worried about them. It's not right, just because they were drug addicts, to let their families suffer by not knowing that they're never coming home again."

"I understand your pain and your determination to make it right somehow. But we can't tell the families what happened without endangering the entire department. But you can honor those people by ensuring something like this never happens again."

Kat knew in her heart that Michelle was telling the truth. To inform the families would be to open up the department to public scrutiny, and for a department that operates behind a cloak of secrecy, that probably wasn't a good idea. "Can we build a memorial somewhere on the grounds? I want to be able to look at it and remember their sacrifice, even if I'm the only person who knows what it stands for."

Michelle nodded, pleased with the idea. "That would be very appropriate. I will get a team on it and of course, we'll want your input as to its design."

Kat nodded, knowing this was the best they could do. It wasn't ideal but it was something. All that remained was to seal the deal.

"Where do I sign up?"

"Welcome to the team," Michelle said, smiling as she shook Kat's hand. "We're honored to have someone like you with us."

Kat released a shaky breath, feeling as if she'd just taken a huge leap toward a new future.

But only time would tell if it was the future she envisioned.

"I don't like it," Jake said when Kat told him of Michelle's offer. "I think you ought to take the identity swap and stop worrying about me."

"Don't be stupid, I would never leave you behind," Kat said, frowning and hurt that he would suggest such a thing after everything they'd been through. "This is a perfect opportunity to take control of our lives. I didn't like the idea of hiding on the run, anyway. This way, I can continue my work without the threat of someone finding out who and what I do, because I'll be in control of all information. It's really the best of both worlds and I can't believe you're throwing a fit about it!"

"You're the one being stupid," Jake argued, unable to temper his words. He was frustrated by his slow progress and feeling damn useless. How was he supposed to provide for Kat when he couldn't remember how he used to make a living? He was barely qualified to be a checker at Walmart much less a government agent, no matter that his job awaited him when he recovered—if he recovered at all. "You have to stop putting your life in jeopardy for me. You need to take the identity swap."

"That's not a guarantee of safety," she countered, her frown deepening. "All it will take is one person finding out that I created MCX-209 and I'll be on the run again, my life in danger with no support or help. This way, I have protection."

"Yeah, from the very people who had tried to force you to make the drug that did this to me," Jake said bitterly. "Doesn't fill me with much confidence."

"Michelle is a good person. She wouldn't make me do anything like Miles did. I trust her."

"Never trust anyone in government," Jake returned darkly, and she cocked her head at him in confusion. He shrugged. "I've been watching a lot of movies lately. I have more spare time than I'm accustomed to."

He was becoming a regular couch potato. Progress was coming but it was far too slow for his tastes. He wanted to remember everything now, not ten years from now. Somehow, even though he was being a royal ass, a warm smile spread across Kat's lips as she surprised him with a cuddle, saying, "It's moments like these that I know I truly love you, because you can be such a pill when you are feeling peckish."

"I am not feeling peckish," he said, his arms wrapping around her instinctually. That settled feeling that followed whenever they touched blanketed his frustration, snuffing it out until he was left with only love for this woman.

"You know you're a terrible patient," she said, gazing up at him. "Surly, cantankerous, uncooperative… the worst."

"I know."

"But even so, I love you, Jake Isaacs."

Her words were a balm to his ragged senses, but he couldn't understand why she'd want to hitch her wagon to his lame horse. "What if I never regain all my memories and I remain this useless waste of oxygen?"

"Stop it," she chastised him. "You're alive and that's what matters. I sleep beside you each night and wake up to you every morning. For me, that's enough. And besides, the rest will come. I have faith. Until then, you're just going to have to get right with the idea that I will be the provider for a while."

"I guess so. Feels weird, though. I feel as if I should be contributing more. I feel like a burden," he admitted.

"Well, you're not," she said, reaching to kiss him on the nose. "You're my knight in shining armor and you will regain your memories because somewhere locked in that brain is the memory of our first time together and that's something you're going to want to remember forever."

He knew she was right. Jake wanted to hold on to any memory involving Kat. She was his world and he never wanted to let her go. Somehow…someway, he'd make his memories come back. Failure wasn't an option.

"Now that we're finished arguing, let's have some makeup sex," Kat suggested with a wink, pulling him toward the bedroom. "I have a new position I found on the internet that I want to try."

Jake groaned with fake fear as he allowed her to drag him into their bedroom. "Careful, you wild woman. The last position nearly crippled me!"

"Oh, stop being such a baby. Don't worry, this time we'll limber up first."

How could you not love a woman like that? He might not remember everything—or much of anything at times—but he knew one thing for sure…Kat was the only woman in the world for him.

And he was just fine with that.

Epilogue

"Jake Isaacs did you take my memory stick again?" Kat asked, exasperated as she searched under countless papers, books and assorted research materials for that tiny mega memory stick for her laptop.

"I don't remember," Jake called out, and Kat followed his voice to see him on the computer, playing yet another brain game. He flashed her a devilish grin and she knew he was teasing her.

"Where's my stick? I need it to finish my notes."

Jake returned to his game. "You are brilliant, you know that? Getting James to do the coding on the games you've created was a stroke of genius. And it works, too. This new game is really charging my batteries. I think I remembered something about my childhood."

"Yeah?" Kat perked up, grinning at Jake. "What was that?"

Jake pushed away from the computer desk and reached out to pull Kat into his lap. She landed with a small squeak. "I remembered that I was never much of a game player unless it was the kind of game involving girl parts and boy parts."

"Oh! Jake, you're incorrigible!" She laughed as he nuzzled her neck. "That is not a recovered memory, it's just part of your DNA. Now, where is my stick?"

"Forget the stick," he said, rising from the chair and dumping her on her feet. "Today, we're doing something special."

"Such as?" she asked as he clasped her hand and pulled her to the garden. "Are you feeling all right?"

"Never better. I have the girl of my dreams—now that I can remember my dreams—and there's only one thing that could possibly make things perfect."

"Being able to remember your birthday?" Kat responded dryly. He graced her with a look that said, *Ha Ha,* and Kat pretended to zip her lips.

"Things looked pretty bleak a few months ago but you were my shining star in a sea of darkness. I knew that you were someone special even if I couldn't quite remember why I knew that. You managed to negotiate a new life for us both, all the while keeping your identity and securing our safety. My memories are slowly coming back—including knowing when I was born, smart aleck—but there's one thing that's still missing and I think it's time to rectify that immediately."

She frowned. "Such as?"

He produced a small black box and she nearly fell over in her surprise. "What is that?" she asked, almost too afraid to know. "I mean, I think I know what it is but I don't want to assume…" She put her fist up to her mouth to stop her babbling. She gazed at Jake, unsure and daring to hope all at once. "Jake? What are you doing?"

Jake's sensual mouth turned up at the corner as he dropped to one knee. He popped the top on the box, revealing a simple yet elegant diamond-studded band and she nearly started bawling right there. "I'm pretty sure I'm asking you to be my wife. Would you do me the honor?"

Was this real? Was this happening? She glanced around their garden, looking for something that might tip off the fact that she was dreaming, such as a unicorn grazing in the cucumbers, and when she saw nothing but ordinary garden fare, she stifled an excited sob to nod vigorously because her throat had suddenly stopped working.

Jake rose and slipped the ring on her finger and that's when she noticed his hands shaking. "I wanted to buy you the biggest ring I could find but then I realized with your work, a giant tabletop of a diamond might get in the way and I didn't want to give you any reason to *ever* take this ring off. So I went with a simple, but gorgeous band of the highest quality diamonds on the market. Do you like it?"

The anxiety in his voice charmed her far more than his usual confidence and she flung herself into his arms. "Yes, I love it. It's perfect."

And it was.

Pretty much everything was perfect.

She and Jake were a team and even if they didn't have all the details figured out—and sometimes Jake couldn't remember the details he'd forgotten—they had each other and that's all that ever mattered.

* * * * *

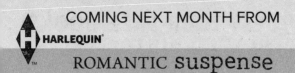

COMING NEXT MONTH FROM

HARLEQUIN

ROMANTIC suspense

Available March 4, 2014

#1791 DEGREE OF RISK
Shadow Warriors • by Lindsay McKenna
After finding love in a war zone, medevac pilot Sarah Benson is taken hostage. Her last and only hope for rescue is her lover, Ethan Quinn. This SEAL will break every rule in the book to save the woman he loves!

#1792 DEADLY HUNTER
Conard County: The Next Generation
by Rachel Lee
When his sweet and stubborn neighbor receives death threats, veteran Jerrod Marquette steps in to protect her. But the closer they get to the truth, the more he falls for Allison, only to discover too late who the real threat is....

#1793 THE ROME AFFAIR
House of Steele • by Addison Fox
Rivals Jack and Kensington find their professional relationship heating up as the two strong-willed security experts go undercover in the Italian wine country to catch a diamond smuggler.

#1794 THE BURDEN OF DESIRE
by Natalie Charles
When a murder victim turns up alive, prosecutor Sally Dawson's career is on the line. She has no choice but to team with her ex Ben McNamara. But is it her error, or a criminal who just may have committed the perfect murder—and won't hesitate to kill again?

YOU CAN FIND MORE INFORMATION ON UPCOMING HARLEQUIN® TITLES, FREE EXCERPTS AND MORE AT WWW.HARLEQUIN.COM.

HRSCNM0214

REQUEST YOUR FREE BOOKS!
2 FREE NOVELS PLUS 2 FREE GIFTS!

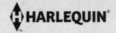

ROMANTIC suspense

Sparked by danger, fueled by passion

YES! Please send me 2 FREE Harlequin® Romantic Suspense novels and my 2 FREE gifts (gifts are worth about $10). After receiving them, if I don't wish to receive any more books, I can return the shipping statement marked "cancel." If I don't cancel, I will receive 4 brand-new novels every month and be billed just $4.74 per book in the U.S. or $5.24 per book in Canada. That's a savings of at least 14% off the cover price! It's quite a bargain! Shipping and handling is just 50¢ per book in the U.S. and 75¢ per book in Canada.* I understand that accepting the 2 free books and gifts places me under no obligation to buy anything. I can always return a shipment and cancel at any time. Even if I never buy another book, the two free books and gifts are mine to keep forever.

240/340 HDN F45N

Name	(PLEASE PRINT)	

Address		Apt. #

City	State/Prov.	Zip/Postal Code

Signature (if under 18, a parent or guardian must sign)

Mail to the **Harlequin® Reader Service:**
IN U.S.A.: P.O. Box 1867, Buffalo, NY 14240-1867
IN CANADA: P.O. Box 609, Fort Erie, Ontario L2A 5X3

Want to try two free books from another line?
Call 1-800-873-8635 or visit www.ReaderService.com.

* Terms and prices subject to change without notice. Prices do not include applicable taxes. Sales tax applicable in N.Y. Canadian residents will be charged applicable taxes. Offer not valid in Quebec. This offer is limited to one order per household. Not valid for current subscribers to Harlequin Romantic Suspense books. All orders subject to credit approval. Credit or debit balances in a customer's account(s) may be offset by any other outstanding balance owed by or to the customer. Please allow 4 to 6 weeks for delivery. Offer available while quantities last.

Your Privacy—The Harlequin® Reader Service is committed to protecting your privacy. Our Policy is available online at www.ReaderService.com or upon request from the Harlequin Reader Service.

We make a portion of our mailing list available to reputable third parties that offer products we believe may interest you. If you prefer that we not exchange your name with third parties, or if you wish to clarify or modify your communication preferences, please visit us at www.ReaderService.com/consumerchoice or write to us at Harlequin Reader Service Preference Service, P.O. Box 9062, Buffalo, NY 14269. Include your complete name and address.

SPECIAL EXCERPT FROM

H HARLEQUIN®

ROMANTIC suspense

Despite the ominous threats she's received, Allison McMann isn't convinced she needs protecting. But her mysterious neighbor, veteran Jerrod Marquette, has other ideas.
The closer they get to the truth, the more he falls for Allison, only to discover too late who the real threat is....

Read on for a sneak peek of

DEADLY HUNTER

by *New York Times* bestselling author
Rachel Lee, available March 2014 from
Harlequin® Romantic Suspense.

"What if someone is still using that poison?" she said as soon as she saw him.

He leaned back against the counter, folding his arms. For the first time she noticed he was armed with both knife and pistol. "My God," she whispered.

He looked down, then looked at her. "I wasn't going out there without protection. Want me to ditch this stuff?"

"Ditch it where?"

"I can put it by the front door with my jacket, or take it home."

She met his inky gaze almost reluctantly. He really did come from a different world. Well, not totally. Plenty of people hereabouts had guns, and some wore them. But somehow this felt different. Maybe because she hardly knew this man and he was in her house?

Still, why this reaction?

Because there was only one reason he would have carried those weapons today. And it explained why he'd eaten lunch with his parka still on.

"I'll go home," he said.

"No." The word was out almost before she knew it was coming. "I'm just surprised." That was certainly true. "I don't have any guns. Well, except for the shotgun in the attic. It was my dad's."

"A moral objection?"

"No. This is gun country. I'd have to object to most of my neighbors if I felt that way. I'm just not used to seeing weapons inside my house."

"Then I'll get rid of them."

"It's okay. Really. This is you, right?"

Something in his eyes narrowed. "Yeah," he said, his voice rough. "This is me. This is me on high alert. I don't need to be on alert in your kitchen."

"I hope not."

Without another word, he unbuckled his belt and removed both holsters from it. The sound of leather slipping against denim, the sight of him tugging at his belt, caused a sensual shiver in her despite the situation. She repressed it swiftly.

**Don't miss
DEADLY HUNTER by *New York Times*
bestselling author Rachel Lee,
available March 2014 from
Harlequin® Romantic Suspense.**

Copyright © 2014 by Susan Civil-Brown

HARLEQUIN®

ROMANTIC suspense

DEGREE OF RISK
by *New York Times* bestselling author
Lindsay McKenna

Love leaves no one behind

Black Hawk pilot Sarah Benson was born brave.
A survivor from the start, Sarah is known for her
risky flights to save lives, and SEAL Ethan Quinn
is just one more mission. But when she needs
rescuing, it's Ethan who infiltrates enemy
territory, and her heart.

Look for the next title from *New York Times*
bestselling author Lindsay McKenna's
Shadow Warrior series, DEGREE OF RISK.

Available March 4, 2014,
wherever books and ebooks are sold.

Heart-racing romance, high-stakes suspense!

www.Harlequin.com

HRS27861

HARLEQUIN®

ROMANTIC suspense

THE ROME AFFAIR
Addison Fox

A Risky Collaboration

It's bad enough that Jack Andrews had once again snatched a plum job away from House of Steele. But now that the assignment has gotten complicated, he wants Kensington Steele to partner him. Danger didn't faze the cool, controlled security expert, but working closely with her mind-numbingly attractive competitor completely unnerves her.

The assignment led them to the Italian vineyard of a diplomat suspected of diamond smuggling. Kensington was determined to keep things professional. But working undercover as a team fanned the flames of their mutual desire. And with a murderer stalking them, the threat to their lives only intensifies the risk to their hearts.

Look for *THE ROME AFFAIR* wherever books and ebooks are sold, available March 4, 2014.

Heart-racing romance, high-stakes suspense!

www.Harlequin.com

HRS27863